Reviews for Martha Egan's Other Titles

La Ranfla & Other New Mexico Stories

"Martha Egan and Papalote Press have put together a seven story collection of enjoyable, readable short fiction. . . . You'll enjoy the heck out of the occasionally bumpy ride in Egan's ranfla suave."
MICHAEL SEDANO, *La Bloga*

"Genuine N.M. characters populate Egan's world. Though the characters in these seven stories are fictional, Egan creates such believable portraits of New Mexicans that you think that they're real people. Neighbors, friends, maybe even family members. . . ."
DAVID STEINBERG, *Albuquerque Journal*

"The seven short stories in Martha Egan's *La Ranfla & Other New Mexico Stories* . . . have a regional base but also deal with situations everyone experiences in one way or the other: how long-standing arguments fade when backs are to a wall; how we learn how to be who we are and also stand up for ourselves; and how a sudden accident or change of plans can set even the most orchestrated life into new motion."
The Santa Fe New Mexican: Pasatiempo

"This collection of stories is packed with human themes of love, deception, generational family ties, cultural confusion, our relationships with animals, all set in the unique cultural surroundings of New Mexico from 1920 to the present. Egan is a marvelous storyteller. She makes you cry, laugh, ponder, and consider yourself in the context of your world, people, animals, and cultural misconceptions. Though set in mysterious environs and filled with indigenous happenings, the universality of her humanity is never muddy to the reader."
Goodreads.com

Coyota

"Egan tells a fast-paced story with plenty of suspense and a well-drawn sense of place; her descriptions of Corrales as well as of Mexico City, San Miguel de Allende, and Guanajuato are a reflection of her long familiarity with the locales."

CANDELORA VERSACE, *Pasatiempo, The Santa Fe New Mexican*

"Egan's descriptive writing is vivid and compelling."

DAVID STEINBERG, *The Albuquerque Journal*

"A gripping thriller all the way through."

Midwest Book Review

"*Coyota* richly illustrates Mexico's charms, foibles, and idiosyncrasies, and the comedy that can result from cultural misunderstandings."

Atención, San Miguel de Allende

"A quick read for a snowy weekend."

CINDY BELLINGER, *Enchantment*

"It is apparent that author Martha Egan, who is an importer herself, is very familiar with Mexico and its culture and the Hispanic culture of the Southwest, of which she writes without sentimentality or clichés. *Coyota* is highly recommended for its vividness and well-crafted plot."

ADRIAN BUSTAMANTE, *La Herencia*

Clearing Customs

"If revenge is a dish best eaten cold, Martha Egan has taken 16 years to freeze herself a vengeful Popsicle of a book."

PATRICIA MILLER, *The Durango Herald*

"Beverly (Parmentier) is one of the most likable characters you will find in a novel. Self-described as 'short, fubsy, and forty-two', she is a returned Peace Corps Volunteer . . . Her quirky characteristics and modesty make you root for her from the very opening pages. . . . The novel (*Clearing Customs*) contains suspense and the feeling of pulling for the underdog."

BRIAN KANE, former Peace Corps volunteer, currently Assistant Director of Admissions, The New School, in PeaceCorpsWriters.org

An Apricot Year

. . . .

Also by Martha Egan

An Apricot Year

A NOVEL

MARTHA EGAN

Papalote Press

Santa Fe

©2012 Papalote Press

Papalote Press
P.O. Box 32058
Santa Fe NM 87594
www.papalotepress.com

ISBN: 978-097558816-1
Library of Congress Control Number: 2011944737

This book is printed on acid-free, archival quality paper.
Manufactured in the USA.

FOR MY SISTER
POLLY EGAN ARANGO
(1942–2010)
a writer in her own right,
who dedicated her life not only to her own family,
but to disabled kids and their families worldwide

"... human beings are not born once and for all on the day their mothers give birth to them, but ... life obliges them over and over again to give birth to themselves."

GABRIEL GARCÍA MÁRQUEZ

PART I

1

· · · · · · ·

LULI RUSSELL PULLED A SABLE BRUSH FROM BEHIND her ear, filled it with paint, and laid down a delicate wash of carmine on a wet piece of paper. She stood back and studied the results. Was the tone a little too blue? Maybe. But with watercolor there was no changing her mind. She added magenta and a touch of white to her brush, then deftly applied the pigment, hoping the result would be a faithful, if impressionistic rendering of the clusters of pale pink blossoms on the spindly tree she was trying to paint. She switched her gaze between the paper and the tree, pleased to see the colors blending together, retaining the individual flowers' details while keeping their overall palette.

Next came the network of branches peeking through the canopy of pink. Against the burnt sienna adobe wall behind the tree they looked black. Closer study suggested lighter shades for the trunk. Its bark was crazed like Raku pottery glazed in shades of Payne's gray with hints of green olive in the creases.

Finches' cheery arpeggios threaded through the faint dissonance of downtown Santa Fe traffic to enliven the clear, bright New Mexico spring morning. Luli was aware of other sounds—jaunty ranchera music playing on a radio next door, the thin strains of a violin floating through the pines up the hill, someone practicing the same measures again and again. The sun lay like warm flannel on her bare arms, the cool mountain air redolent with the aromas of ponderosas, junipers, and espresso brewing somewhere nearby.

As the sun warmed her, Luli paused to take off her fleece vest and toss it over a chair. "Hooray! Painting outside in a T-shirt. In April. I'm not in Green Bay anymore." She returned to her painting with renewed focus. This was her sixth study of the morning and she was beginning to experience the joy of finally getting it right.

At precisely that moment, the phone rang. "Dammit," she muttered. "Can't you see I'm busy?"

Absently, she reached across the drawing board for her cell phone, upsetting the jar of water she used for washing out her brushes. In horror she watched the dirty water flood the glass topped table, heading for her paintings, while her teenage daughter's voice came wailing through the phone.

"Oh, my God, Mom, you have to come home right this minute," Jenna pleaded. "I'm, like, so weirded out? I can't stand it."

Luli pressed the phone to her ear with one hand while frantically trying to stop the spreading pool with a wad of paper towels in the other. "What's the matter, sweetie? Has something happened to your father?"

"That SHIT! I hate him. Please come home, Mom, please, please? I need you."

Luli took a deep breath and summoned her most soothing voice. "Jenna, get hold of yourself and tell me what's going on."

"Stupid fucking Paula DeCleen!" Jenna shrieked. "She's such a total twat. I was driving her to school this morning, me being a nice neighbor to that dimwit BITCH, and she's, like, 'Is it really true your Dad's shagging Darleen Renard?'"

Luli stopped breathing.

"And I was, like, 'No way.' But she said she saw them having a majorly smoochy dinner at the Players' Club last week. And then, late last night? When Paula's mother picked her up from work at McDonald's? They saw Dad's car parked in Darleen's driveway, and she goes, 'There weren't any lights on in her apartment'."

"Oh, how silly, Jenna. Darleen Renard? Absolutely ridiculous. It must have been somebody else's car."

Even as Luli attempted to dismiss Paula's gossip with smooth platitudes, a big screen image popped into her head: melon-breasted, bleached blonde Darleen Renard, the family's former babysitter, grinning stupidly at the camera, clutching a leering Herb close to her bulging chest. It was true. She knew it. Darleen and Herb had always been too chummy. It had been a good enough reason for her to hire a new babysitter ten years ago.

"Honey, settle down. Please? This could all be a big mistake."

"C'mon, who else drives a powder blue Cadillac with a vanity plate that says 'Big Herb', huh? It was him, for sure.

He didn't come home last night either. He left me this note that was, like, 'I'll be in Milwaukee overnight on business. Don't wait up.' The whole town knows where he really was. Lying sack of shit! I hate his fucking guts."

"Jenna, your language."

"Would you please wise up? I'm talking about your husband? My father? Cheating on you big time in front of God and all of Green Bay, and you're, like, quibbling about my vocabulary? Jesus, Mom."

Suddenly, the sun was blistering. Luli felt faint, black spots pulsating behind her eyelids every time she blinked. She stopped trying to salvage her work, collapsed into her chair, and inhaled deeply.

"I'm sure there's an explanation. Maybe they were out with a group of people, and Herb left his car at her place. Or maybe he loaned his car to a friend of hers. I don't think it's fair to your father to make such assumptions, Jenna."

"Fair? Hello? Which planet do you live on? Do you think he cares about what's fair to me or you or any of us? How fair is it that I have to put up with a screaming imbecile like Paula DeCleen sniffing around my family's dirty laundry?"

"Really, sweetie, I think you're being overly dramatic. I'll call you this evening when I've had a while to think this through and maybe talk to your father. In the meantime, I expect you to put in a good day's work at school."

"No way! I'm not at school, and I am not going back there, OK? I dropped off Paula the Dork and came home, and this is where I'm staying. Can you imagine what she's telling the whole school, that blabbermouth? I can't stand this. I hate him. I am totally never going to talk to him again ever," Jenna sobbed.

2

· · · · · · ·

LULI FLIPPED THE PHONE SHUT AND LAY HER HEAD down on the patio table, its glass surface cool against her forehead. Stunned and numb, her heart turning to ice, she thought back to her fiftieth birthday party at the Baird Creek Country Club in Green Bay just a few weeks ago. Herb had reserved a table by the bay window overlooking burnt umber fairways dotted with patches of snow, like mini icebergs moored in a sea of dried grass. The sky was a polar blue seemingly poised to melt into the frozen creek winding along the bottom of a birch-lined hillside. Luli recalled the pristine white of the linens, the gleam of silver and crystal, the smiles of her radiant daughters and good-looking twin sons assembled around the table, beaming at her. Her husband, in a rare display of family pride, puffed out his chest like a rooster about to crow.

At the end of the meal, their waiter brought out a cake bristling with candles, and Luli's family sang "Happy Birthday." The other servers and the entire dining room joined in, clapping, cheering, and whistling.

Luli's face was flushed, and not solely from the glass of red wine she'd had with her steak dinner. For a few minutes she was speechless, embarrassed by the attention. It wasn't like Herb to make a big deal of her birthday, although it was her fiftieth. "Thanks, guys," she managed to say half under her breath, "but you might have told them to go easy on the candles."

Herb laughed, pecked his wife on the cheek, and presented her with a fat white envelope. "Happy Birthday, honey."

"Open it, Mom," Jenna said.

"Yeah, open it," the others chimed in.

Luli swept her smooth, streaked blonde hair back from her face. Using a table knife, she slit open the envelope, put on her reading glasses, took out a few of pieces of paper, and gave them a quick glance. She was puzzled. "Artisan? Is this some kind of arts organization? Are we giving them a donation, Herb? I've never heard of them."

"Mom," Allie said. "Geography quiz—which famous art center and capital city have you always dreamed of visiting?"

Luli's jaw dropped and her large amber eyes grew even wider. "Santa Fe. I'm going to Santa Fe? Why?"

Herb rolled his eyes. "Look at the other stuff in the envelope."

She unfolded another page. "A voucher for a month's stay at Casa las Rosas," she read aloud. "A charming, well-appointed territorial adobe a mere three blocks from the Plaza in the heart of historic Santa Fe."

Perplexed, she put down the pieces of paper and looked around the table at her grinning family.

"There's more. Open this one," Jenna said, handing her a box wrapped with shiny paper and sparkling ribbons tied in an oversize bow.

Luli ripped the paper off the wooden container and lifted the lid. Inside she found a half pan set of 48 Schmincke watercolors, beautiful little cakes of paint, each one individually wrapped like expensive chocolates. The box also contained a fat Arches watercolor block and three Winsor Newton Series 7 sable brushes.

Luli took off her glasses, her eyes misting. "Herb, I can't believe this."

Herb shrugged. "Believe it, honey."

"Are you coming with me?"

"No, I've got a lot going on right at the moment with my new shopping center in De Pere. I'll join you later for a few days." He smiled at his astonished wife and cleared his throat. "Well, isn't this what you've always been yammering about? Going to the Southwest, doing your art thing? Your dream come true?"

Allie groaned. "Dad, you are such a romantic guy. What he means to say, Mom, and can't quite articulate more graciously, is that this is our present to you for all your years of taking care of us, cooking for us, cleaning, driving us around, helping Dad run his business. Basically, you've put your own life on hold for twenty-eight years. It's your turn. It's high time you got to do something for yourself."

"We all pitched in," Paul said, indicating his siblings, who nodded in unison.

"Of course, I helped out," Herb said. "In fact, the whole shebang was my idea."

Luli looked around the table. Jenna, the youngest, the one who looked the most like her, with the same thick straight blonde hair, but her father's green eyes. Allie, her eldest, serious, studious, thoughtful, her eyes brimming with tears behind horn-rimmed glasses, her chin propped up on her palms. The twins, Paul and Jeff, tall, sturdy young men with wide shoulders and wide smiles, a little uncomfortable in the formal dining room's fragile chairs, but very proud to be her sons. Herb, most of his hair gone now, his once handsome face furrowed with worry lines, his athlete's frame slumped into a paunch. All of them beaming as if they'd hit a hole-in-one.

"Almost like a real family," she thought. "If only for a moment . . ." Luli shoved aside ugly memories of the years of protecting her children and herself from Herb's drunken rages—the mental as well as physical abuse they all feared.

3
· · · · · · ·

LULI LIFTED HER HEAD FROM THE TABLE IN SANTA FE and discovered the paintings she'd spent the morning working on were unsalvageable. All her concentration and skill, now hopelessly mired in a drying puddle of murky water. Her entire body quivered. She was terrified. She was filled with rage. Her brain seemed to have run aground on a pile of sharp rocks, and she felt a headache coming on. Then a familiar reaction to disaster kicked in: hunger. She was ravenous, especially for something sweet and goopy, and a huge latte. She went inside the condo, grabbed her purse, and slammed the kitchen door behind her. The tree full of finches that had been serenading her from an overhanging box elder sprang into the air and flew away in a whirring squadron.

Luli's hulking, slime green Ford station wagon, the mom mobile her kids called "Mrs. Phlegmish," took up most of the narrow driveway. She stabbed a key at the lock several times, the clump of keys clanging against each other like wind chimes as she spat out her fury in an increasingly loud voice. "Fucking son of a bitch! What an idiot I've been! For years I've put up with his crap, his laziness, his sleaze, his put-downs, his drinking, his temper. And yes, his violence. His affairs I thought were simply flirtations. How could I be so fucking stupid? And this is my reward?"

After a half-dozen thrusts at the lock, the key hit its mark and slipped into place. She slid into the front seat, turned on the ignition, and gunned the engine. It responded with the mucousy roar that had earned the car its nickname. Luli jerked the gearshift into reverse, and the car leapt backwards, spitting gravel on the stucco wall beside the driveway.

In a swooping arc, she backed onto Otero Street, nearly colliding with a Range Rover rapidly descending the hill. The boxy car, California plates fore and aft, screeched on its brakes just in time to avoid hitting her. Its young male driver flipped her the bird and zoomed on down the hill. Luli stopped in the middle of the street and took a deep breath. "Slow down and be careful," she told herself, as if she were talking to one of her teenagers. "On top of everything else, you don't need to wreck the car."

She gently put Mrs. Phlegmish into drive. Luli Russell was a cautious, sensible person—or at least she used to be. This morning she felt as reckless as a drunken frat boy. In fact, she was so out of control she scared herself. "If Herb was here and I had a shotgun, I'd blow his goddamn brains out," she thought. "Lucky for him, he's far away, back in Green Bay. Shacking up with the delectable Darleen," Luli snarled out loud, startling the driver of a car facing her across the intersection.

Like pieces of a puzzle falling into place, Luli realized she had Darleen Renard to thank for Herb's wonderful birthday present. "That conniving bastard! That amoral slut! They deserve each other."

Her thoughts drifted back to the evening of her birthday party. When they returned home, the kids went upstairs to sleep or read or fiddle around on their computers. Herb poured himself a generous Scotch from the dining room sideboard.

"This trip to Santa Fe will be a well-deserved, special time out for you, honey. It's high time we did something nice for you, after all these years of you being a wife and mother."

And, Luli thought, an unpaid bookkeeper in your construction business.

"Maybe you'll get rich and famous so you can pay me back for all those painting lessons I footed the bill for."

"Herb, dear, you'll recall I paid for those lessons myself. Loren thinks I have a lot of talent."

"Loren? Oh, you mean Mr. Pansy Decorator? I always thought he mainly wanted to get into your pants."

"Loren's a friend, Herb, and he's gay. He's not interested in me. But he has sold some of my work."

"So what? Maybe he swings both ways. Sure, he hung your paintings up in his gallery. Maybe he bought 'em himself."

"He sold three of my paintings to the Citizens' National Bank in December. They're hanging in the president's office. Maybe you saw them last time you went in for a loan."

"What's that supposed to mean?" Herb said angrily. "My relationship with the bank is none of your goddamn business, so shut the fuck up!"

"Oh, Herb, please. We had such a lovely evening, our children, the gifts, the beautiful dinner. Let's not argue."

"So let's kiss and make up."

Standing behind her, he began nuzzling her neck, shoving his hips against her backside, reaching his arms around to squeeze her breasts. The drink sloshed all over her blouse. He put it down.

"Herb, I'm not in the mood," she said softly, hoping the kids wouldn't hear. She covered his hands with hers and moved them to his sides.

Herb encircled her chest again, grabbing her more tightly. Luli tried to squirm out of his grasp.

"Jeez, give a guy a break, will ya? I've put out a bunch of money for this big birthday deal. Time for you to put out for me, huh?"

Luli wanted to say, "Allie told me after dinner that she and her sibs scraped together their own money for the watercolors and the trip to Santa Fe. They saved up for more than a year—almost a thousand dollars—not you." But the important thing was to ease away from him without provoking an outburst.

"Herb, please? Don't ruin this for me."

"Don't you ruin it for me, you frigid bitch!" He slapped her hard on her bottom. "You haul your fat ass upstairs or I'll plug you right here and now."

Luli started to run away but Herb was right behind her. He grabbed her wrist, stopped her, and pushed her against the wall. Changing his tone, he began to plead, whispering softly, breathing whiskey in her face. "Aw, come on, Luli, show me a little affection for a change."

"Herb, you're drunk, and you know how I feel about that—you're not attractive to me when you've been drinking."

Herb's face grew redder still. "Oh, yeah, Miss High and Mighty? Ask me if I give a rat's ass about your . . . *feelings*." He cocked his arm back like a pitcher and swung at her with a closed fist. Luli ducked and ran into the library, locking herself in.

Herb began to pound on the door and yell. "Let me in, you bitch! You open up pronto or you'll regret it!"

"Hey, Dad?" a deep, male voice called down from the top of the stairs. "Leave Mom alone, would you please? C'mon, it's her birthday, for Chrissakes."

"Who the fuck do you think you are, Paulie, telling your old man what to do?"

"As a matter of fact, I'm nineteen. I'm a football player who outweighs you by about thirty pounds of muscle—not flab. And I'm a head taller. News flash: You are never going to lay a finger on me—or my brother, or my sisters, or my mother—ever again." He started down the stairs to underscore his point.

"Oh, yeah?" Herb's words were slurred and he swayed, holding onto the library doorknob for support.

"Yeah, Dad. Your days of using your fists to show us who's boss around here are finished."

Jeff came to the head of the stairs, followed by his sisters.

"We're done, Dad," they said. "Go to bed."

"Or we're calling the cops," Jenna added.

Herb spun on his heels, flung open the front door, and stormed out of the house, slamming it shut with a loud bang.

4

· · · · · · ·

DRIVING DOWN PASEO DE PERALTA, LULI WONDERED
if Herb had deliberately sabotaged her wonderful birthday
present. Did this mean her dream of having time to paint,
of becoming a professional artist, was going up in smoke?

During the years of her marriage, Luli was rarely able
to indulge her lifelong passion for art. Sure, she'd painted
the children's rooms with murals of meadows and cows and
barns when they were little, but she seldom worked on her
watercolors.

Herb always resented the time she devoted to art—the
classes she took at St. Norbert's; the gallery openings at
Loren's; her once a month get-togethers with pals for plein
air sessions in a park along the Fox River—when it wasn't
twenty below. Her "studio" was a corner of their dank,
chilly basement. She'd be preparing paper for a new painting, or adding details to a sketch she had been working on,
or totally lost in an intricate watercolor, when Herb would
clatter down the steps and ask her when dinner would be
ready, or if she'd iron a shirt for him, or where his car keys
were. His going along with their kids' idea of sending her

to Santa Fe on a painting holiday astonished her. It was an uncharacteristic, unbelievably generous gesture, in fact.

Yeah, it was unbelievable, all right. She banged the steering wheel with the heel of her hand. Sneaky, arrogant shit! How had she not seen through his ruse? Herb wanted her away from home so he could diddle his girlfriend and probably line up his ducks to divorce her—Luli, the mother of their children, his "life partner," as he stated sarcastically when he was drunk. "That shithead! That jerk! Twenty-eight years of wedded bliss and I'm out on the street like last week's garbage."

A block down Paseo, she drove past the Pepto-Bismol pink Scottish Rite Temple heading toward the Palace Swiss Bakery on Guadalupe Street. If there ever was an occasion for a calorific splurge, this was it. A triple latte and a sugar and butter-laden pastry, preferably involving chocolate, might bring her comfort momentarily, even knowing how guilty she'd feel afterwards.

Luli waited in a seemingly endless line to pick up her coffee and a couple of sweet rolls that probably ran three thousand calories each. Once she was back in the Ford, with her paper coffee cup securely wedged between her purse and the bag of bakery goods on the front seat, she decided to stop at Kaune's grocery on Washington Avenue for a *New York Times* and a bottle of milk. She turned into the parking lot, only to realize the store wasn't open yet. But, there was a bank of newspaper vending machines. As she fished in her pockets for quarters, she heard a loud groan from the far side of a rusted-out pickup next to her car. She froze. She heard it again. A low, guttural sound followed by short cries of pain. She darted around the truck.

On the ground beside the pickup, a gaunt, greasy-haired old man in filthy clothes lay on the asphalt, curled into a fetal position. Bright red blood trickled from the side of his mouth, his watery blue eyes spun in wild panic, his body shook and jerked. Luli shrieked and dropped her coins, frantically looking around for someone, anyone, to help her.

The only person in sight was a groundskeeper raking leaves in front of the bed and breakfast across the street. She waved her arms and hollered to catch his attention. "Mister—help! Help! There's a man here—he's bleeding badly."

The yardman dropped his rake and came running. Luli led him around the truck where he fell to his knees beside the writhing, moaning old man, and in what looked like a practiced move, touched his fingers to his neck. "Ay, dios," he said, glancing at the man's pale, sweaty face, his closed eyes. "Low pulse. We gotta get him to the hospital fast. No time to wait for an ambulance."

"Quick, into my car," Luli said. "It's right here."

She flung open the back door of the station wagon. Together, they scooped up the bleeding man and laid him down gently on the back seat. Luli floored it and peeled rubber out of the parking lot.

"God, I don't even know where the hospital is," she wailed over her shoulder.

"Go left onto Paseo and then left again at St. Francis," he directed in a calm, steady voice. "I'll guide you from there."

Luli screeched around slow-moving cars, weaving in and out of traffic, honking her horn, earning angry insults from other drivers.

The yardman cradled the injured man's head in the crook of his arm and murmured words of encouragement. "Easy, hombre," he said, patting his chest gently. "You're gonna make it. I'm a medic, and we got you covered, amigo. Stay with me. Please hang on." He took a kerchief out of his pocket and tried to mop up the blood dribbling out of the injured man's mouth as he coughed and sputtered.

Luli sped up when she saw the hospital ahead. With a squeal of rubber, she braked to a stop at the ER entrance and flew in the double doors. In minutes, white-coated orderlies followed her outside, pulling on latex gloves, and wheeling a gurney. They carefully lifted the bleeding man onto it and whisked him into the hospital.

Luli and the yardman followed, watching the gurney and the attendants disappear behind swinging doors into the triage area. They looked at each other and exhaled almost simultaneously. Luli touched his sleeve. "I don't know what to say," she said, "except thank you."

The man smiled and shrugged. "Don't thank me. You found him and got us here really fast. My name is Adán Alire, by the way. I'd shake your hand, but I don't think I better," he said, looking down at his blood covered hands.

Luli laughed nervously. "I'm Louise Russell. Everyone calls me Luli."

A hospital clerk approached holding a clipboard. "I have a number of questions I need to ask you about the patient."

Luli and Adán looked at each other. "We don't know him," Luli said. "I found him lying in a parking lot, and Mr. Alire came to help. Judging from his clothes, I'd guess he's indigent."

The clerk sighed. "Well, I have to ask you your names and a few questions anyway, if you don't mind." She noticed Mr. Alire's bloody hands. "And you'd better have somebody check you out," she said with a slight frown.

"I'm fine. It's his blood, not mine. I'll go wash up."

"But you should see somebody first," the clerk said, signaling to a young nurse wearing a stethoscope and latex gloves. She examined Mr. Alire's hands and forearms, asking if he had any cuts or open sores. A stricken look clouded Adán's face.

"We routinely screen for HIV," she explained. "I doubt there's a problem, but please leave your name and a phone number with us. We'll call you as soon as we have the victim's blood test results."

"I'm sure you're all right," Luli said, patting Mr. Alire's shoulder. "But I never thought about that."

"Me neither," Adán said, regarding his blood splotched denim shirt and jeans. "I'll go wash up and call my wife. I'll be right back."

Luli wandered the waiting room, stopping at a picture window looking out onto the hospital parking lot and the purple mountains beyond. She breathed deeply to calm herself, wondering what was going on behind the ER's closed doors. Would the man live? She didn't think he'd been stabbed. His bleeding seemed more like some kind of hemorrhage. She felt chilled, her clothes damp with cold sweat.

In no time, Adán reappeared, smelling of soap. He had washed, rolled his sleeves down and buttoned the cuffs, but his clothes were still stained with blood.

"Would you like me to drive you home so you can change?" she asked.

"We live up off East Palace, but I can walk home from where you picked me up, if it's more convenient."

"I'd be happy to take you to your house. I think it's close to where I'm staying."

They returned to the Ford, parked haphazardly in the ER lot. Adán put Luli's purse, an upturned paper cup, and a coffee stained bakery bag on the floor, slipped into the passenger side, and looked into the back seat. "There's a lot of blood on your upholstery, Mrs. Russell."

"It's Luli. I don't care about the blood. I hate this car."

Adán looked at her in surprise. "Still, it'd be a shame to ruin the upholstery, since it's kind of a new car and all. My wife probably knows how to take out bloodstains."

Luli drove slowly out of the hospital parking lot. Abruptly, she steered Mrs. Phlegmish to the side of the road and burst into heaving sobs that convulsed her entire body. When she could compose herself, she wiped her eyes and nose with her sleeve. "I apologize, Mr. Alire. It's been quite a day so far, and it's probably not even 10 a.m. Could you give me the tissues out of the glove compartment?"

He passed the box to her. "Don't worry. I'm a little shook up myself. That was quite a wild ride, and to tell you the truth, I wasn't sure the man would make it to the hospital alive. His pulse was almost zero and his heart was fluttering like a butterfly's wings." He gazed out the passenger window. "Well, we did the best we could for him."

5

· · · · · · ·

ADÁN DIRECTED HER TOWARD THE CENTER OF TOWN and uphill to a circle of traditional flat-roofed houses scattered across a knoll like a jumble of cardboard boxes. Brilliant yellow daffodils and golden forsythia marked the flagstone walkway leading to the Alires' neat adobe, half-hidden behind shade trees just beginning to leaf out.

As Luli parked the Ford, a diminutive, round-faced woman with short, curly dark hair strode briskly out the front door toward them, wiping her hands on her pink plaid apron. Luli stood waiting beside the car while the woman wrapped her arms around her husband's waist, and rested her head against his broad chest. He draped an arm across her narrow shoulders.

"Mrs . . . um . . . ma'am, this is my wife, Rosealba."

Rosealba smiled and took Luli's hand gently in hers. "You're a very brave lady. I'm happy to meet you. Won't you please come in for a cup of coffee?"

Luli started to decline the offer, but the thought of a hot cup of coffee coursing through the coldness inside her was irresistible. As she followed the couple into their home she found she was shaking. She wasn't sure why—whether from the cool morning air, the race across Santa Fe with the injured man, or the emotional shock of the morning's news. In the dark interior, she was instantly reminded of her mother's house in pretty, verdant Wrightstown, Wisconsin, where she grew up: the mingled scents of candle wax and lemon oil, the red and yellow oilcloth-covered kitchen table, the tan and gold-speckled Formica countertops, the vintage avocado Frigidaire in the corner, and the hint of delicious spices in the air.

But looking around the kitchen—the cacti on the windowsill, the little wooden plaques painted with saints, the red cupboard recessed into the adobe wall with its cutout border—Luli began to feel lost. The Alire's swishy-sounding Spanish and the Latino oompah music on the radio brought her back to Santa Fe, far, far from home. Here she was in a strange house in a town where she didn't know a soul, among people who lived in another language, another culture. This beamed, low-ceilinged house wasn't really anything like Mother's roomy, sunny, wallpapered clapboard farmhouse after all. Luli regretted accepting the invitation. She should have gone directly home to her condo. Who were these people and what was she doing here in their home?

She crossed her arms, tucking her frozen hands into her armpits to warm them, and sat down gingerly in the straight-backed pine chair Adán held out for her.

"Why didn't somebody else find that man?" she thought.

Herb would have been furious with her for going to his rescue. "You're constantly embarrassing me, butting into other people's business," he had told her more than once. "I'm only trying to be helpful," she'd counter. Even now she could hear his scorn. "Well," she thought, "Herb Russell is a selfish bastard and a coward and I don't care what he thinks of me anymore. I did the right thing."

Rosealba gathered cups, saucers, spoons, and a plate of homemade cookies, and chatted as she made coffee. "Are you from around here?"

Luli shook her head. "Wisconsin."

"Wisconsin," Rosealba mused. "Isn't that where your cousin Luis lives, Danny?" she asked her husband. "I call him Danny. Even though his name is Adán—Adam in English. His mother calls him Adán. Our niños call him Pops, our grandkids call him Papacito. He answers to all four and just about anything else—unless of course, there's a basketball game on TV, and then he don't answer to nothing but maybe a call to nature," she giggled.

Adán smiled shyly, and shifted in his chair. "Luis is in Chicago, mi amor. Illinois is the state south of Wisconsin. He goes up there fishing sometimes, though."

Rosealba poured the coffee. But as she pulled out a chair to sit down, she noticed Luli's hands shook when she reached for her cup. "Pobrecita, you're cold, aren't you? I'm gonna go find you a shawl."

Luli set her cup down on its saucer with something of a clatter and protested. "No, really, Mrs. Alire, I'm fine."

Rosealba had already disappeared, returning in seconds with a rainbow-colored afghan she wrapped around Luli's shoulders.

"You've had a big shock. Of course you're cold. I wouldn't have had the courage to do what you did."

"I didn't do anything but yell for help. It was your husband who came running. He knew what to do—I didn't."

"You could have ignored that man. A lot of people would have. But you didn't. And you took him to the hospital in your car. Danny says you drove like el diablo mismo, exactly like them crazy New York taxi drivers we see on TV. If that guy lives, it's because you acted fast."

Luli started to praise Adán again but an uncontrollable flood of tears spilled down her face. Rosealba jumped out of her chair and enveloped Luli in her arms.

"I'm sorry to be so emotional. Really. It's been a pretty shocking morning." Unable to stop herself, she told the Alires about Jenna's hysterical phone call from Green Bay minutes before she happened upon the bleeding man.

"I can't believe my husband is doing this to me and our children," she sobbed. Then she got a grip on herself. "Oh, please forgive me. I'm not myself. I apologize for laying all this on you."

Adán stood up, and patted her shoulder. "You're going to be all right. It's probably all a big misunderstanding. It's nothing to be embarrassed about." He disappeared down the dark hallway off the kitchen to change his clothes.

Rosealba held out the coffee pot.

"No more coffee for me, thank you, Mrs. Alire. It was exactly what I needed, but I'd better be going." She pushed her chair back.

"Now, Mrs. Luli, I don't mean to intrude, but are you going to go home alone to your casita after all this? I want your phone number where you are so I can call you tomorrow to be sure you're doing good."

Luli was a little taken aback, but she wrote her number down in the gingham bound notebook Rosealba placed in front of her.

While she wrote, Rosealba opened a broom closet and took out a bucket, rags, a box of salt, and a pair of rubber gloves. "Before you leave, let's see if we can do something about them stains on your car seats," she said briskly.

"Oh, Mrs. Alire, that's not necessary," Luli protested. "I can take care of it myself later. Really."

"No, no." Mrs. Alire shook her head, filling the bucket in the kitchen sink as she drew on the gloves to protect her small, heavily veined hands. "This is something I can do. I think you done your part. Todos unidos en la lucha."

"Excuse me?"

"Oh, you probably don't speak Spanish. It means we're all in this together."

"I got A's in Spanish in high school. But I don't think I learned much."

"Remember 'vamos'"?

"Didn't the Cisco Kid always say 'vamos' when he jumped on his horse?"

Rosealba shrugged. "I don't know that one. We didn't have no TV when I was a kid. Vamos—let's get to work." She turned off the faucet, slung the heavy pail out of the sink, and bustled out the back door.

Knowing it was useless to protest, Luli followed.

"Eeeeee, this is a nice car," Rosealba crooned. "OK—where are them bloodstains?"

Luli showed her the dark red smears on the floor and the back seat.

"This isn't too bad," she said, climbing in. "I hate to tell you, but I seen worse." She tossed the floor mats out onto the driveway. "Here—give these a bath. There's a broom by the back door and a hose bib along the side of the house. If you run water on these mats and swish the broom around on them, the blood will come right off."

She sprinkled salt on the bloodstains on the seat and began rubbing at them gently with a soft cloth.

"OK, Mrs. Alire."

Rosealba leaned back on her heels from her perch on the floor and looked up at Luli. "Please call me Rosealba. I'm not some old lady, you know. I mean, aren't we about the same age?"

Luli reddened. "Well, yeah, probably. I graduated from college in '71."

"So maybe," Rosealba said, furrowing her forehead in concentration as she dumped on more salt. "Let's see, I would have finished high school in '67. If it hadn't been for . . . well, you know . . . m'ijita, Rose. My first one. I guess you and I are about the same cosecha, . . . about the same year." She laughed and returned to her task, faintly humming a tune Luli didn't recognize.

Luli fetched the broom and carried the plastic mats to the flagstone under the faucet, turned on the water, and while she scrubbed, she inwardly berated herself. "Here's this wonderful welcoming, warmhearted woman. She probably thinks I'm putting on airs, talking about when I went to college. Why didn't I say I was born in '50 instead? I sound like such a snob!" The dark red stains bled thin streams of pinkish water and vanished along with her self-reproach.

Rosealba appeared with a paper coffee cup and a soggy bakery bag drooping from her fingertips like wet laundry. "What should I do with these?"

"Oh, my breakfast. The coffee must have spilled."

"All over the seat. But I got it. And your purse too. Good thing it was leather, not some kind of cloth. All I had to do was wipe it clean. I don't think no coffee got inside it."

"Thank you so much. I guess in all the confusion I completely forgot about the pastries I bought at the bakery."

Rosealba inspected Luli's Blackwatch skirt. "Nope, doesn't look like no coffee got on you."

"That's because I got it all over me," Adán laughed as he walked toward them in a clean chambray shirt and pressed jeans. "The coffee soaked through from the spill, I guess. Looked like I'd wet my pants. I threw them and my shirt into the machine and put them to soak in cold water, mi alma," he said to his wife, kissing her lightly. "I'd better go before they fire me. I'll see you around five."

"If you can wait a couple of minutes until we finish, I'll give you a ride," Luli said. "It's on my way."

"No need to wait. We're all done," Rosealba said. "Looks like brand new. It's such a beautiful car. I love this color green. It reminds me of my jade plant."

"You're finished already?" Luli said.

"Sure. The upholstery's coated with that Scotchguard stuff. It really works. You go on, honey," she said to her husband. "Oh, but don't you want your breakfast?" Rosealba held up the dripping bag.

"Toss it," Luli said.

As if by magic, a big, raggy, spotted dog ran up the driveway and slid to a stop at Rosealba's feet. He sat back on his haunches, panting, looking up with huge watery eyes at the soggy white bag, and licking his chops.

"Ayyy," Rosealba shook her head. "Your timing is always perfect. Luli, this is Basura—it means garbage. And that's what he lives for. Adán found him at the dompe. You are what you eat, right, Basura?"

The dog barked his agreement. Rosealba tipped the bag and dumped out the pastries. The dog caught them both expertly in his mouth and dashed off around a corner of the house, disappearing as fast as he had appeared. Everybody laughed. Luli and Adán climbed into the station wagon, and slowly drove the rutted road toward downtown.

That night, Luli called her daughter Allie in Boulder to give her the bad news. "Maybe if I'd lost fifteen pounds and taken better care of myself, dyed my hair or something, he wouldn't have wandered."

"Totally not true. You look terrific, Mom. Women pay a ton of money to have their hair streaked like yours is naturally. You have a great figure, perfect teeth, clear skin, and a beautiful smile. You're a Viking princess!"

"Uh, not exactly, dear."

"And you're hot. Guys are always giving you the eye—even ones half your age. Haven't you noticed? You don't look anything like fifty."

"Your father's always telling me I'm fat and I have a big ass."

"He's the one with the fat ass, since he never gets any exercise—except for bending his elbow, of course."

"Well, he does play golf."

"Golf is not exercise. You might as well walk around your front yard and swing your arms a few times. Golf is really about hanging out in the country club bar—at least in Dad's case."

Luli sighed.

"You are not fat, or wrinkled—but he is. Putting you down is his way of controlling you."

"Controlling me?"

"Yes. Especially now we're grown ups, maybe he's worried you'll dump him."

"So he beat me to the punch."

"That's a possibility. Anyway, looks have nothing to do with what happened. Dad's going through male menopause. Taking up with a brainless bimbo like Darleen. The family babysitter. Doesn't he know that's a cliché? It's fucking pathetic."

"For this subtle analysis, you're getting a Ph.D. in Psychology?"

"I'm glad you can joke about it. You're far better off without him. We all are. He has always been totally self-centered and smug, like he's the king and we're his dimwitted vassals. I hate it when he does his 'I'm so brilliant and you're so stupid' put-downs. But after he started getting plastered and smacking us around . . . I really don't care if I ever see him again, the asshole."

6

. . . .

TRUE TO HER WORD, ROSEALBA CALLED THE NEXT morning. "How are you doing today? Why don't you come over later? I'll be home from my house cleaning job about 4 o'clock."

Luli accepted.

When Rosealba opened the door, Luli was greeted by the scent of something delicious in the oven. "Ooooh," she said, her eyes wide. "What's cooking?"

"Nothing special. A pie. Apple. But it's not quite ready yet. Let's go sit outside. It's such a nice day."

The women sat at a round table on sun-faded metal lawn chairs from the 50s under a flowering tree. The spring afternoon was unusually warm, the sky a clear, deep cerulean blue, the sun gentle on their shoulders. Rosealba served tall glasses of pink juice.

Luli took a sip. "This is delicious. What is it?"

"Agua de sandía, watermelon juice. It's easy to make. I'll show you how."

"Wonderful." She took another sip. "Thank you for being so kind to me yesterday, Mrs. Alire. Please forgive me for crying on your shoulder."

Rosealba waved off her apology. "Mrs. Luli, we all have days when nothing goes right. As Adán always reminds me, 'No todo en la vida es miel sobre tus hojuelas.'"

"Translation, please?"

"Not everything in life is honey on your cornflakes.'"

Luli laughed. "That is so true."

"But, yesterday was a really, really bad day for you! With your husband making trouble, and your daughter home alone. And finding that sick old man. Things will get better for you and your family. You'll see."

Luli looked up into the gnarled tree shading them. Its light pink blossoms looked familiar. In fact, she realized, they were like the ones she'd been painting the morning before. "I know this isn't an apple or a pear; I grew up with those in Wisconsin. What kind of tree is this?"

"It's an apricot. Isn't it pretty? Adán planted it for me when we got married. So far, so good this year."

"Why do you say that?"

"You have to be an optimist to plant an apricot tree in Santa Fe, although almost everybody's got one. At the first sign of spring, the silly things flower, like now. We have to start crossing our fingers. If we have a hard frost before the fruit sets, we don't get no apricots. Since we're so close to the mountains here, it can snow into mid-May, and that's what usually happens. We maybe have a crop every five years if we're lucky."

She looked at Luli, and her eyes lit up. "Something tells me this is gonna be an apricot year. If it is, by the end of

July we'll be up to our ears in them fruits. Apricot empanadas, apricot pies, apricot preserves, dried apricots, agua de albercoque. If I'm right, we'll be giving them away by the zillions."

Rosealba jumped out of her chair. "¡Ay dios! My pie. I hope I didn't burn it." She ran into the kitchen.

Luli sipped her juice, enjoying the peace, studying the tree shading her until Rosealba reappeared with hot slices of apple pie topped with cinnamon ice cream.

"Wow."

"Eat fast, Mrs. Luli. It's melting."

"This may be the best thing I've ever eaten in my life."

"And don't worry. It hasn't got no calories. I took 'em out."

"What a pleasant way to spend an afternoon. It's been years since I sat in a backyard like this with a friend. When I was growing up in Wisconsin, people had time for each other. Not any more."

"I forgot to ask, what brings you to Santa Fe?"

"All my life I've loved to paint, but I rarely had time. When I turned fifty, my children gave me lessons at Artisan on Canyon Road, a set of special watercolors, and a stay in a lovely one-bedroom rental on Otero Street. Yesterday, I was painting a little tree with these same flowers. But yours is huge. It's like sitting under a big pink cloud."

"Come by here tomorrow and paint it."

"I'd love to, but I should pack up, go right home to Green Bay, and take care of my daughter, Jenna. She is so upset."

"I thought you told me she could stay with her granma."

"True. They're great pals. I wasn't supposed to go home for another week. Maybe a few more days will give us all a chance to calm down."

"She can take care of herself. You come over and paint this tree. Them flowers don't last long. You see something beautiful like this, you gotta enjoy it while it's there."

At first, Luli was uncertain of accepting this woman's offer of friendship. They had led such dissimilar lives, they could have been from different planets. Their backgrounds, their educations, their family life, their frames of reference, language—nothing was alike.

She had to wonder, if Rosealba had been alone and friendless in Green Bay, would she have welcomed her into *her* house?

Luli set up shop on the metal patio table in the Alire's back yard, creating one study after another of the gloriously flowering tree. When Rosealba came home from work, she watched Luli finish a painting.

"There's one thing I know for sure—your husband ain't no art critic. These are beautiful. It's magic watching you swirl those colors around until they look exactly like apricot flowers. I could never do that in a million years."

"I want you to pick one out. Your favorite. Hang it on the wall to remind you of how beautiful your tree is next time there's an off year."

"Really? I can have one?"

"Sure. In fact, take two or three. I've painted a half-dozen."

Luli and Rosealba had wonderful chats, talking about experiences they had in common as mothers, the news, whatever they felt like sharing. Rosealba made Luli feel taken care of, safe, protected, at home. There was something unusually warm and comforting about her soft voice, her melodious English, her genuine concern as she listened thoughtfully while Luli tried to sort out her new situation.

On her way to the patio, Luli noticed an entire wall of the living room hung with family photographs. "Wait. Before we go outside, would you tell me about all these pictures?"

"Of course," Rosealba said. She took down a photo of a smiling teenager in an army uniform. "This is our Lonnie," she said, gazing lovingly at his image. "We didn't want him to enlist. Adán, especially. When my husband was eighteen, he volunteered for Vietnam. Signed up as a medic, thinking he could go to medical school later on the GI Bill, but that war wrecked his life. His best buddies got killed right in front of him, he got malaria over there in Cambodia—and he never even made it to college. Them fevers still come back. They're why he can only do the garden work, and sometimes not even that.

"Anyway, when Lonnie was fifteen, an army recruiter at his high school talked him into signing a piece of paper saying he'd join up when he turned eighteen. They didn't tell us. After he graduated, he didn't really want to go no more, but he thought they'd throw him in jail if he didn't. We couldn't do nothing about it. The recruiter told him they'd train him to program computers. Lonnie loved computers. Instead, they made him a truck driver. He was killed in the first Iraq War."

Rosealba's golden brown eyes darkened and lost their customary gleam. She took a handkerchief out of her apron pocket and blotted them.

"I think about him all the time. I miss him so much. We all miss him. He could make you laugh even on a really, really bad day."

Luli put her arms around Rosealba and pulled her close. "How tragic! I don't think I could survive losing a child."

A few moments later, Rosealba lifted her head and smiled. "After some time passes, you feel so glad you had him for those years—it helps ease the pain. Our other kids are doing great. We have so much to be thankful for."

One by one she pointed out her children. "This is my Rosie on her wedding day. She's married to a wonderful guy—they have their own construction business. They've got two hijos. My oldest grandbaby is Daniel. He's six. And his little brother Renzo's four. Those are their drawings on the refrigerator. I love my hijitos to death and spoil 'em rotten."

She handed Luli a photograph of a young man straddling a shiny motorcycle with a pretty girl behind him.

"This is my daughter, Beatriz. With her boyfriend, Joe. She's studying to be an RN at UNM. He's a motorcycle mechanic. They've known each other since kindergarten. They're living together in Albuquerque, but they're getting married in late summer, after Bea graduates.

"Here's our youngest, Arturo. He had a rough couple of years after Lonnie was killed—they were real close. But he pulled himself together and now he's a sophomore at UNM, studying electrical engineering. He got a full ride scholarship. So did Beatriz."

"You must be awfully proud of them."

"We are. You can meet them, real soon I hope. Do you have pictures of your family with you?"

"I certainly do." Luli opened her purse, took out a pocket size photo album. "This is my eldest, Allie. This spring she's getting her doctorate in psychology in Colorado."

"She's real pretty, and she must be smart. She looks a lot like you."

Luli smiled and flipped a page. "These husky football players are my twin boys, Paul and Jeff."

"Twins? They don't look nothing alike."

"They're fraternal twins—two eggs. Their personalities are very different. Paulie's kind of serious, and Jeff's a comedian."

"My Lonnie was, too. He liked to play tricks on us. Are your boys in college?"

"Yes. They're at the University of Wisconsin—sophomores like your Arturo. I wish I could say they're majoring

41

in something as serious as engineering, but frankly, I think they're majoring in football and girls."

Rosealba laughed.

"This is Jenna; she's the youngest. She wants to be an oceanographer."

"She looks real sweet. Is she the one who called about your husband?"

"Yes. She's an excellent student. Sometimes too emotional for her own good. And not always all that sweet, to tell the truth."

"Well, girls sometimes are more trouble than boys. But I don't blame her for being upset."

"Me neither. This mess is more than a teenager can handle by herself."

Luli turned another page to a fading Polaroid with a scalloped edge, stopped, and gazed wordlessly at the photo.

"Who's the little blonde girl in the black and white photo? Is that you, Luli? And who's the good looking guy standing beside you?"

"Yes, it's me. I was about eleven when my dad took this picture. That's my older brother, Nat. He went to Vietnam and was killed a week before he was supposed to come home."

Rosealba shook her head in dismay and hugged Luli. "You've had your losses, too."

Luli nodded. "He was my pal. I couldn't talk to my mother very well, and my dad . . . well, he was either at work or in the bars. Nat was a great listener. I could tell him everything. He taught me to drive when I was ten."

Rosealba's eyes widened. "Ten?"

"Yeah. We had lots of farm roads where I grew up, dirt roads, no traffic. I still can't believe he's gone," Luli sniffled. "He had all these great plans for when he got out—get a Master's degree in counseling, marry his longtime girlfriend. Then a mine blew him up. And for what? Nobody has ever succeeded in explaining Vietnam to me, why so many fine young men like Nat had to die or come home crippled. And think of how the Vietnamese people suffered—hundreds of thousands killed, their entire country destroyed, poisoned."

"Them awful wars. I don't understand why we have to fight people we don't know way on the other side of the world."

"It makes no sense to me either."

7

· · · · · · ·

VAN BUREN PHILLIPS WAS HAVING A DREAM. A TERRI-fying dream that started out pleasantly enough. He was standing on the terrace of a lovely villa, holding a tall, cool, refreshing drink, gazing over a broad expanse of water. Was he on the Cape? No—there were palm trees and sea grapes, and the ocean was a clear, variegated aquamarine sparkling like jewels. Somewhere on the Italian Riviera? The Adriatic? No, he realized, a shudder of dread coursing through his veins, as the scene became clearer. No, this was his house on Sainte Foi in the Leeward Islands, the seaside cottage that had been his family's second home for years. He, his wife Sylvie, and their two sons often spent their vacations here. He recognized the blue gingerbread trim beneath the roofline, the huge, terracotta water jars at each end of the terrace to collect runoff from the pitched roof. Yes, it was most assuredly their house.

He was having that awful nightmare again. Running through his head over and over like a horror movie he couldn't turn off.

The scene opened in gaudy Technicolor with the sun melting into the ocean in a blast of tropical fruit colors, a thin grenadine film spreading out across the water's surface, casting a rosy glow over the stippled seascape of gentle waves rolling toward him. Then, thick black clouds rolled in. The picture grew hazy.

For the thousandth time, Van Buren saw himself on the veranda fronting the ocean. He was dressed in his usual costume: white slacks, a white Lacoste polo shirt, a navy blazer, and Top-Siders. He was leaning on the veranda's iron railing having a drink. A sundowner. God, it tasted good. A Myers's and soda. Or maybe it was a planter's punch. Something sweet, chilled, and potent. The ice cubes knocked against his teeth as he tipped the glass back and drank a long delicious draught, soothing his thick, parched tongue. Except it turned molten as he sipped it, the raw effluent of alcohol permeating the delicate membranes of his gullet, his sinuses, engulfing his head, his stomach in biting fumes. As he coughed to clear his throat, a gush of blood spewed up his esophagus, filling his mouth. Burbling, free-flowing blood. Trying desperately to wash away the warm metallic taste, Van Buren gulped hungrily at his drink, taking larger and larger swigs until he was swallowing without tasting it, seeking to quench the fire with the potion searing his insides.

As he guzzled, angry voices drew his attention down to the beach where his sons, Luc and Henri, stood grappling with one another in a wildly rocking rowboat a hundred feet offshore. The boys were tugging at each other's clothing, punching each other. They were always fighting about something, those two. Cain and Abel. When Henri, the younger one, grabbed a fistful of his brother's hair and yanked hard enough to throw the older boy off balance, Luc jerked an oar out of its oarlock. Henri did the same, and soon, they were jousting. Van Buren tried to yell at his sons to put the oars down, but only a faint groan came out of his mouth. He was going to run to the shore and demand they stop fighting. But his glass was empty. He'd go deal with them in a minute. After he poured himself another drink. It would scarcely take a second. Maybe Sylvie would like another one. Where was she?

Then he remembered. Sylvie wasn't there. Not in the kitchen. Not in her bedroom with one of her headaches. Not in the cottage anywhere. Nor was she down the coast in the little pink house they'd rented for her mother, Françoise. No, Sylvie was gone. The tennis pro said he needed to give her more lessons, and she went to the hospital with him so she could work on her backhand and her serve. A hospital in Switzerland where everyone wore tennis whites, and spoke French, and where they wouldn't let you have cocktails. He didn't need to fix her a drink after all. Just one more for himself.

Knowing where the dream was leading, Van Buren tried desperately to stop it. Shutting his eyes more tightly didn't help. The film continued to roll on in lurid, tumultuous color. As his heart began to drum, he watched a strange crowd of people amass along the water's edge at the bottom of the cliff. In a cacophony of French and English, they began to shout and gesticulate toward a point offshore. Van Buren recognized some of them—people he knew from the yacht harbor, his Wall Street firm, a couple of his classmates from Yale, the doorman from his Park Avenue apartment building, Sylvie's father, who had died right after Luc's birth. They were all screaming. In the water, men were dragging something pale and heavy toward shore. A dolphin? A fish? When they came out of the ocean, he could see it was a limp body they laid down on the sand. One by one, all the people looked up at him on the terrace and angrily shook their fists.

He did his damnedest to find his way off the porch, frantically running from one side to the other, searching in vain for a way through the iron railing, but there was no gate. He tried the French doors leading into the house, pulling on them, banging on them, but they were locked and none of the servants came to open them. He yelled for the people below to help, but everyone ignored him. They didn't seem to care that Van Buren needed to reach his boys. To convince them to stop fighting. To tell them brothers should be friends. He was going to enforce the rule once and for all: you never stand up in a small boat. It could tip over. And somebody could get hurt.

Van Buren tried to climb up and over the terrace railing, but someone was shoving him back, pushing him down onto hard pavement, pebbles grinding into the back of his head and shoulder blades. He couldn't see who it was. He fought to open his eyes, but they seemed to be glued shut.

When he tried to raise his hands to his face to pry open the lids with his fingers, he found he couldn't move his arms. Van Buren struggled blindly to stand up, but his legs didn't work. Something or somebody was holding him down. He grew increasingly frenzied. His heart thrumming at a frantic pace, he fought to get to his sons. His boys needed him. Maybe one was already injured. Sylvie would be furious if he didn't intervene. She'd blame him if anything happened. "One day, they'll really hurt each other, Van, if you don't do something."

Blind and paralyzed, Van Buren tried to fight against the unseen force pushing him into the asphalt. As he heard someone—a woman—yelling for help, he lost consciousness.

His eyes flickered open and shut. He was moving. Or in something that was moving, lying on his back. Everything hurt. A man he didn't know was looking down at him, urging him to hang on. "I'm a medic," he said. Van Buren was mystified. He'd never been wounded. He'd never been in a war, or even in the Army. A black curtain fell and he couldn't open his eyes again.

When he regained consciousness, he was at least lying on something softer than pavement. A masked figure in pale green was prying his jaw open, shoving a hard pipe down his throat. It hurt like hell. He tried to fight, but he didn't have the strength. Henri's angry face floated before his closed eyes. Or was it Luc's? One of the boys was shoving an oar down his throat. That must be it. As best he could, Van Buren pleaded with him to stop. But Henri kept pushing the oar further and further down his father's esophagus, tearing at the membrane, making him bleed. Blood filled Van Buren's mouth as he fought for breath, his heartbeat grew weaker and weaker, a fading, sputtering outboard. Now he couldn't move his arms or legs at all. He felt like someone had strapped him down. A searing, shooting pain radiated out from under his ribs threatening to consume him, as if his innards were all on fire. Then Henri, his face skewed in anger, stabbed something sharp into Van Buren's arm and everything went black.

PART II

· ·

8

. . . .

THE DRIVE TO WISCONSIN WAS DISHEARTENING. LULI had five days to go on the condo rental and several classes left, but she needed to be home, especially for her daughter. The car was loaded with her clothes, her paintings, her watercolors, and the gifts she'd bought: chile ristras for her friends' kitchens; a case of hot sauce for her kids, who preferred the stuff to ketchup; a set of green and white cactus glasses and matching fruit plates for the cottage in Door County; two necklaces of delicate strands of melon shell and turquoise for her daughters' graduation presents. Other boxes and bags of souvenirs that didn't seem to matter any more, since her treacherous husband had shredded the fabric that had held her family together.

She guided Mrs. Phlegmish along highways leading northeast, putting Santa Fe and the Sangre de Cristo Range in her rear view mirror. With every mile closer to Green Bay, she felt as if she were climbing up another rung of a tall, shaky ladder, and the burden of an unknowable future weighed heavier and heavier on her. Her fears threatened to throw her off balance, setting her up for a long, hard fall. What was she going to say to her husband? To her children?

Her mother? Her friends? Father Van Laanen? Divorce was something you read about in *People*. Something that happened to celebrities—not to a nice Catholic girl like Luli Russell, a woman who had always done what was expected of her as a daughter, a mother, a member of her community, and most especially, as a loyal wife.

Adán Alire said maybe it was all a big misunderstanding. But his wife's look told Luli what she and any woman knew in her heart of hearts to be the truth. When your husband hustles you out of town, and takes up with a woman half your age, and you hear about it from your daughter, who herself hears about it from her classmates, you're the last to know. This was no misunderstanding. This was Pearl Harbor, and the whole fleet was in flames.

Two-and-a-half days and thirteen hundred miles later, after countless hours of driving through the rain-dreary, unplanted fields of Kansas, Iowa, and southwestern Wisconsin, Luli steered her land boat off the interstate and onto Green Bay's well groomed, tree-lined streets. Like an old nag returning to her barn, Mrs. Phlegmish loped up the driveway to the Russell's two story, 70s brick house tucked into a grove of tall, swaying pines, and came to a lurching stop in front of the garage door painted with an outsize oval "G" in Packer green and gold.

Luli frowned seeing Jenna's vintage Buick Skylark parked on the left side of the driveway. In the paneled library, she found her youngest child sprawled on the sofa staring at the TV, wearing a T-shirt and flannel pajama bottoms, a half-eaten bowl of popcorn perched precariously on her bare stomach. Jenna lifted her head when her mother stood between her and the screen with her hands on her hips.

"Mom? I thought you were in Santa Fe for another week. What are you doing home?"

"I think that's my question, young lady. What are *you* doing home in the middle of the afternoon on a school day?"

Jenna sighed heavily, set the popcorn bowl down on the floor, and sat up slowly. She pulled her threadbare T-shirt down over the wide elastic waistband of her pajamas, and sat hunched on the edge of the sofa, chewing the ends of her honey blonde hair.

Luli sat down and put her arms around her daughter's shoulders, drawing her close and kissing her lightly on the temple. Jenna couldn't look at her mother.

"Why aren't you in school?" she asked gently, tucking Jenna's hair behind her ears.

The girl's eyes brimmed. "It's no use. Dad was like, 'There's no money to send you to Scripps next year, so forget about it.' Besides, I can't face the other kids. Everybody knows. School totally sucks."

"That's not like you at all. You've always loved school." Luli hugged her daughter and fought back her own tears. "Look, we're going to get through this, Jenna. You are going to Scripps. I don't want you to worry or even think twice about it. We'll figure it out. It's not the end of the world."

"He's such a total shit. Why didn't he at least wait until I graduated? Did he really blow all our money? Like Grandma says he did?"

Luli's head came up off her daughter's shoulder with a jerk, but she suppressed the wave of panic swamping her. "Let's not jump to conclusions. Give me a second to catch my breath. Remember, I just got here five minutes ago. I never should have left. None of this would have happened if I'd stayed home and paid more attention to what was going on right under my nose."

"Oh, Mom, that's soooo not true. You can't blame yourself. I think he's been screwing her for years. Asshole!"

"Jenna, don't talk that way. He is your father no matter what. Where is he anyway?"

"He left early this morning. Said he was going to Fond du Lac on business. Everybody tells me they see his car parked at Darleen's apartment at all hours. He's probably there at this very moment fucking that skank. I so totally hate him. Why did he do this to us? Why is he wrecking our family? Why won't he go into rehab? Toby's mom did, and she's fine now."

Luli sighed. How was she going to deal with such a mess? "Did he say when he'd be home?"

"Around dinner time? I think he expected me to cook for him. Like, I'm his personal kitchen slave or something? Dogshit burgers! Cat turd lasagna! Totally the kind of dinner I'd like to fix for him. It's all I can do not to sprinkle Drāno on his corn flakes in the morning. He knows

I know. It's been beyond awful without you here. Grandma's wonderful, but she has her own life, her job, church stuff, bridge club, plus it's a forty-minute drive each way to Wrightstown. Dad doesn't even bother coming home at all some nights. Oh, Mom, I missed you so much." Jenna curled tighter into her mother's arms, sobbing.

Luli took a deep breath. Then, like the sun breaking through storm clouds, a smile lit up her face. "Jenna, dear, let's prepare a special reception for your father. When we're done we can go have dinner at the club. After almost three days of greasy, tasteless road food, I'm dying for one of their big, crunchy chef's salads. How does that sound to you?"

Jenna looked up at her mother and was astonished to see her smiling. "What kind of a reception do you have in mind, Mom?"

Luli opened a bottle of pinot grigio, poured two glasses, and passed one to her daughter. "Time to clean house." She threw open Herb's closet and swept all his ties into her arms. "Let's hang these off the front door knob. And these shoes! He's the only guy in town who still wears two-toned shoes. Toss 'em on the lawn."

At first, Jenna stood by in silence watching her mother root through Herb's closet like a burrowing ground hog. Soon the girl got into the swing of things, hurling his belongings out the front door.

"While we're at it, can we get rid of his totally embarrassing plaid golf pants? They're, like, totally butt-ugly."

"Yes, indeed. And the plaid sport coats and the lime green polyester pants. Jesus, what a fashion sense this man has." She pulled out the drawers of his dresser and dumped their contents on the floor. "Toss these shiny black nylon socks. I hate them, especially when he wears them with Bermuda shorts and boat shoes."

Jenna gathered up the plastic trophies on her dad's dresser. "How about these?"

"Absolutely. Especially the 1968 blue plastic UW water-skiing prize he's so proud of. He would never have won it except there were high waves on Lake Mendota that afternoon and all the other competitors fell in."

In the dining room, Jenna took half-empty bottles of cheap whiskey out of the sideboard and added them to the ever-expanding pile of clutter on the lawn. From the kitchen she retrieved cans of anchovies, sardines, Vienna sausages, and Spam. "I don't know he can stand to eat this crap."

"Me, neither," Luli said with a grimace. "Yuck-o."

Giggling, mother and daughter flung Herb's possessions onto the grass.

"We forgot his golf clubs," Jenna said.

"How could we? And the buckets of *balls*. You know, the day you were born, I had to ask our eighty-year-old neighbor, Mrs. Jennings, to drive me to the hospital. Herb knew I was in labor when he left that morning, and my babies usually popped right out. But he had an important golf date 'with an investor,' he said. He didn't show up at the hospital until five hours after you were born, and then he was plastered."

"I never knew that."

"Well, you didn't need to know it."

When they had piled most of Herb's worldly goods in front of the house, they stood back to survey their handiwork, howling with laughter. Heaps of clothes, cans, bottles, shoes, golf clubs, crossing guard orange and acid green practice balls were strewn all over the dead grass.

"Ah, I just thought of something else," Luli said. She went into the house and emerged with a pair of shears. One-by-one she gathered up the ties hanging on the doorknob and cut them in half. "Let's go eat. I'm famished."

"Wait, we forgot his absolutely most prized possession."

Jenna dashed into the house and reappeared tossing a football. She held it steady in her outstretched hands. "I have always totally wanted to do this."

"Oh, Jenna, dear, maybe you shouldn't. Maybe the boys would like to have that ball. Or your sister. She's the most rabid Packer fan in the family."

"Tough. Don't forget Dad smacked me around, too."

Luli watched in amazement as Jenna expertly drop-kicked Herb's 1966 Super Bowl football signed by all the Packers, including Coach Vince Lombardi, over the neighbor's cedar hedge, and into the Klug's swimming pool.

"Touchdown!" Jenna cried, raising both fists in the air.

9

· · · · · · ·

THE RUSSELL HOME WAS DARK. NIGHT HAD FALLEN, and a single spotlight shone above the garage door. Short, stocky, and red-faced, Herb Russell stood in the drive- way beside his baby-blue Cadillac Seville. He scowled as he watched Luli park her car next to his without making eye contact. She pushed down the power locks. With Jenna wide-eyed in the passenger seat, she sat motionless behind the wheel, looking straight ahead.

Herb's heavy brogans slapped the pavement angrily as he stomped up to his wife's car and stood by her par- tially opened window. "What the hell is going on here?" he demanded in a rage, gesturing toward the disarray on the lawn. "What the fuck do you mean, ruining my ties and throwing my stuff all over the yard, huh?" He pulled on her door, trying to open it. "And why is the house locked up? We never lock this house. You know I don't have any keys to this place. I want you out of this car right now."

"Go inside, Jenna," Luli said quietly, giving her the house keys. "I'll see you in a few minutes. Your father and I need to talk."

Without so much as a glance at Herb, Jenna ran up the steps and disappeared into the kitchen, firmly closing the door behind her.

No sooner was his daughter out of earshot than Herb Russell began to yell at his wife, his face twisted in anger.

Luli didn't move. Herb reached through the window, but she shoved the power button forward and it clamped shut on his forearm, holding it tight in its glass jaws. Yowling with pain and indignation, he began to kick at the driver's side door. He pounded on the window with his left hand while trying to wriggle his right one free. Luli eased the window down until he could drag his arm out, then immediately ran it up again.

Clutching his wounded limb tenderly and wincing, Herb hissed through his teeth. "You fucking bitch. You've got a helluva lot of nerve locking me out of my own goddamn house and embarrassing me in front of my neighbors."

"Oh, are you embarrassed, Herb? Gee, I thought I was embarrassed. Your children and I. Jenna especially, since she's the last one still at home."

Herb set his jaw and narrowed his eyes to knife slits in his raw red face. "Give me the fucking house keys, and go pick up my shit."

For several minutes, Luli studied the garage door as she rested her arms on the steering wheel. "I think you're forgetting something, dear," she said, turning to face her husband squarely through the almost closed window. "You don't live here anymore."

"The fuck I don't!" he screamed. "This is *my* house."

"Actually," she said calmly. "Not any more it isn't. It's my impression you've made a choice to live someplace else. In fact, I hear you've got a nice, homey situation on the West Side."

"Says who?" Herb snarled.

"Oh, everybody in town. Now, why don't you toddle back to your tacky, pretentious car and go home to your slutty little mistress like a good philanderer."

Herb exploded, kicking the door and pounding the windows with his fists, hurling epithets and threats at his wife, who sat staring stonily ahead as her husband's blows glanced off the Ford's tough epidermis. Up and down the street, porch lights flicked on and curtains parted as the neighbors watched Herb pummel his wife's car and bloody his fists.

In the distance, a police siren sounded faintly. As it grew louder, Herb stopped flailing at the solid car and straightened up. A look of disbelief spread across his face.

"My neighbors are calling the cops on me?" he said half-aloud to himself. "Or my daughter?"

A police car stopped in front of the Russell house, and a tall, burly man with thick, straight blond hair combed back from his chiseled features stepped out. He strode across the littered lawn toward the station wagon, one hand on the butt of the billy club swinging from his belt.

"'Evening, Herb," the policeman said in a gentle voice that belied his impressive size. "Something wrong?"

Herb chuckled laconically, tucked his sore, battered fists into his pants pockets, and smiled broadly at the policeman. "Jerry Bourgoin, my man," he said cheerfully, rocking back and forth on his heels. He extended a hand in a friendly greeting, trying not to wince when the policeman clasped it in his strong grip. "Long time no see. How's it goin'? Hey, the wife and I were having a little disagreement, that's all. I don't know why anyone would have called you. No need to bother an important officer of the law like yourself over a piddly little private deal between a guy and his old lady, don'tcha think?"

Jerry didn't reply. As he approached the station wagon, Luli lowered her window. Their eyes met—a warm, familiar meeting. She gave him her hand. He took it in a gentle, lingering squeeze.

"Thanks for coming, Jerry. How've you been?"

The officer smiled shyly. "Super, Luli." A subtle grin teased the tanned skin at the corners of his mouth into deep parentheses. Facing Herb, he pulled himself up to his full six feet five inches, jingling the coins in his pants pocket. "Y'know, Herb, maybe it'd be a good idea if everybody gave it a rest for a while."

Herb stiffened. He looked up at the policeman and shifted his weight from one foot to the other. "What do you mean, Jerry?" he snapped. "I think you're forgetting something. This is *my* house. *My* wife. *My* business."

Jerry nodded thoughtfully, his large brown eyes inspecting the ground by the toes of his spit-polished, size thirteen shoes. "Well, probably you ought to spend the night some-place else, Herb," he said softly.

Herb spun around and stomped off toward his car. He flung the Seville's door open, jammed himself behind the wheel, slammed the door shut, and screeched backwards out of the driveway. Jerry watched him, his eyes onyx glints. He motioned for Herb to slow down, and the Seville jerked to a stop in the middle of the street. Herb nodded at the cop, flashed him a cheesy, sarcastic smile, put the car into first, and eased down the street at an exaggeratedly slow pace.

Jerry sighed. Luli got out of the Ford, hugging her-self, her legs quivering. Leaning against stalwart Mrs. Phlegmish, she and Jerry watched the Seville slowly disap-pear around the corner.

"Same asshole he ever was," Jerry said. "Hasn't changed a bit since high school, has he?"

"Nope. I shoulda known better."

The policeman nodded and rubbed his jaw. "Are you gonna be all right?"

"Thank you, Jerry. Yeah, my daughter and I will be fine." Luli exhaled slowly. "He's embarrassed himself enough for one evening. Would you like a cup of coffee or a pop?"

"Not right now, thanks. Do you want to file a com-plaint?"

"No, he won't be back. At least not tonight."

"You're probably right. Well, gotta go. I'm due at the sta-tion." He took a pen and a notepad out of his breast pocket and wrote down a number. "This is my cell phone," he said, ripping out the slip and pressing it into her hand. "Anytime, Luli, anytime. OK?"

"I appreciate it."

They stood side by side for several minutes, looking in opposite directions, deep in thought. Luli smiled. "Say hi to Tina and your kids from me. And tell your wife she's a verrrrryyyyy lucky woman."

Jerry grinned. "I tell her that every day," he said, laughing as he strolled toward his patrol car.

10

· · · · · · ·

WHEN LULI RETURNED TO WISCONSIN IN WHAT SHE considered disgrace—or at the very least acute embarrassment—her neighbors and pals gathered around. They called her up, stopped by, invited her to lunch, took her shopping or to work out at the gym—activities they used to enjoy doing together. But all of her women friends were married. Even if the spouses were miserable and ill suited to each other, people in Green Bay didn't divorce. It was obvious to Luli that her break-up with Herb had created a divide between her and the women she thought she was close to. They now seemed uncomfortable around her. They never mentioned Herb or her children. Their upbeat attitude seemed forced, phony. She had to wonder, were they afraid infidelity and divorce were contagious? The truth was, in lily white, upper middle class Midwestern society, a woman who couldn't keep her husband happy and hold her marriage together was a loser. The failure of Luli's marriage was just that—a failure. Her failure.

Luli had to brace herself for the calls from her divorce lawyer and the accountant.

"I hate to be the one to have to tell you this, Mrs. Russell," the accountant said, "but your husband . . ."

"Former."

"Your former husband has, as they say, taken you to the cleaners."

"I beg your pardon?"

"It appears the assets you and your, er, former husband accumulated in your quarter-century of marriage are gone. In fact he has emptied all your bank accounts."

"But what about the savings account for the children? To go to college?"

"Gone, unfortunately."

Luli felt like she'd been kicked in the stomach.

"Then there's the portfolio. All sold. Mostly at a loss, I see. Singularly unwise of him. The house, of course . . ."

"What do you mean, 'The house, of course'?"

"Why, he took out that equity loan last fall. Surely you knew about it?"

"Excuse me?" She tried to level out her voice, not to sound shrill. It wasn't working. "This is a community property state. I didn't know anything about an equity loan. This house is paid for."

"No, actually, the loan amount was quite substantial. And apparently your husband applied the money to his shopping center project in De Pere. We'll have to look into that. Hmmm. This appraisal can't be right. Anyway, you'll have to put the house on the market, I'm afraid, . . ."

The discussion dragged on for another fifteen minutes,

a litany of financial disaster. By the time Luli could hang up, she was breathless and horrified. Her mother was right. Herb had blown all their assets. Shortly after their confrontation in the driveway, he left town with his girlfriend, allegedly heading for Florida—leaving his wife and children fielding calls from his angry creditors and nearly penniless.

Father Van Laanen, the family's longtime parish priest, called and asked if he could stop by. "Word must be out," she thought.

She served the grizzled old man coffee and watched as he dumped half the sugar bowl into his cup.

"How is your relationship with Herb?" he asked.

"Over. He has taken off with . . . with a much younger woman. And I'm quite certain it isn't the first time he's been unfaithful."

The priest looked down at his scuffed wingtips. "Well, these misunderstandings happen. He'll be back."

"I hope not. He cleaned out our bank accounts, he's in debt up to his eyeballs, and we've had enough."

"Louise, please don't do anything hasty. For your sake and that of your family."

Father Van Laanen was the only person aside from her mother who called Luli by her formal name.

"The kids and I have been talking it over, Father. We're divorcing him."

He shook his head sadly. "Louise, can't you find it in your heart to forgive him? To be more compassionate? Men do . . . men do these things. I know it's not right, but . . . Perhaps God is challenging you to be more generous with your husband. He's testing your willingness to accept Herb's frailty."

Luli was outraged. "Herb hasn't asked for my forgiveness—or for his children's. He has treated us with brutality for years, abandoned us in a very public manner, left us destitute, and humiliated. We're losing our home because of his selfishness, his . . ."

"Trust in the Lord, Louise. He will bring your husband home to you."

"Father, I know you mean well. But I don't want him back. If the Lord sends Herb home to us, I hope it's in a hearse."

Luli drove to Wrightstown to have lunch with her mother.

"I don't want to shock you, but the kids and I have decided to divorce Herb."

"I'm not surprised, after his awful shenanigans," Mrs. Alberts said, laying crisply ironed linen napkins beside matching placemats on the dining room table. She fetched two neatly arranged plates of tuna salad from the kitchen, and sat down across from her daughter, regarding her through sparkling blue trifocals. When she folded her perfectly manicured fingers together, Luli noticed her nail polish and her lipstick were the same shade of coral pink. A matching barrette held her smooth white hair back from her face.

Mrs. Alberts cleared her throat. "I'm incensed that he would do something so heinous to you and my grandchildren. I've tried to appreciate my son-in-law all these years, I truly have. But Herb Russell has never been the kind, thoughtful, good provider I wanted for you. You will recall I tried to talk you out of marrying him."

"Yes, I admit I was a fool not to listen to you. What can I say? I was young and stupid. And, well, pregnant."

"I told you I'd help you. I didn't care about that."

"But I cared about it. I didn't want to embarrass you and the whole family. Besides, Herb was thrilled. I truly thought I was in love with him. We'd known each other since high school. I didn't like him then, but in college when we started dating, he was fun. He was my best friend. He seemed so sincere. He even recited poetry—Kahlil Gibran and Rod McKuen. Awful stuff, but still, I was touched. No guy had ever paid so much attention to me."

"I could tell you were getting serious about him by your junior year. Remember? I tried to convince you to date other men."

"By then Herb and I were a habit. We slid into spending all our time together: studying, meeting for meals. We spent weekends together—although I refused to sleep with him. I was sort of in his slipstream, and I never went out with anyone else.

"I can't believe how stupid I was the night he seduced me."

"I'm not sure I need to know this, Louise," Mrs. Alberts said, focusing on her plate.

"Hear me out," Luli said, waving her fork in the air. "It's about time we talked about this. It's been almost thirty years, after all. Herb had just gotten an 'A' on an English term paper—which I wrote for him—and he invited me out for a steak dinner to celebrate. On his mother's credit card, of course. After he lost his baseball scholarship for poor grades and failing to show up for practice, he couldn't even afford to take me out for a hamburger on his own nickel."

"His mother always overindulged that boy. He was her only child," Mrs. Alberts said sorrowfully. "I guess she felt she had to compensate because he never knew his father. Fred's plane went down in Korea, you know, and his body was never found."

"Herb kept ordering piña coladas for me while he drank Cokes. Said he was staying in training—for what, I don't know, since he'd dropped out of all his sports. I woke up in his bed in the morning wondering how I got there.

"I knew right away I was pregnant. When I told him the test results, he was beside himself. The first thing he said was, 'Sayonara, Vietnam!' Then he asked me to marry him."

"Do you think he got you pregnant on purpose?"

"Well, I knew he was adamant about not getting drafted. Having a wife and child was his way out of the war."

"Does Allie know she was an . . . early . . . baby?"

"She certainly does. All along, I've told my kids the facts of life in terms they could comprehend. I especially don't want my girls to make the same mistake I did. And I want my boys to behave responsibly."

"Have you talked with Father Van Laanen?"

"He came by yesterday. I guess everyone in town knows about our family debacle. His advice about Herb was to 'forgive' him and take him back when he's ready. Total garbage! Like the advice he and the other priests gave you about putting up with Dad."

Mrs. Alberts looked down into the lap of her navy blue floral print dress and sighed.

"Then I had the most amazing revelation. The minute he left my house, it all went poof. The mystical body of Christ, the virgin birth, indulgences, papal infallibility, the resurrection, transubstantiation, mortal sin, heaven, hell, limbo. The whole song and dance. And the pagan baby thing— how did we ever buy into that? Not only am I divorcing Herb, I'm divorcing the Catholic Church."

Mrs. Alberts groaned. "Even though I don't believe in divorce, you and the children will be better off on your own, especially after this . . . indiscretion of Herb's. But why leave the church, Louise? Your faith can help you weather the worst of storms. I can tell you that from experience. Your father tested me sorely many, many times."

"Yes, he did. He wasn't always wonderful to his offspring either, as you will recall. What did Father Van Laanen and the other priests tell you?"

"That he was my cross to bear. That I would get my reward in heaven."

Luli took a deep breath. "Can I ask you something?"

Her mother tensed. "Certainly, dear."

"Why didn't you leave Dad?"

Mrs. Alberts looked away, gazing out the picture window, set her fork down on her plate, and steepled her fingers in front of her face. "Why, I had you children to look after. I . . . wouldn't have been able to support us."

"Your parents wouldn't have helped you . . . us?"

"You never knew your grandmother. She was a very hard-hearted woman. A strict Irish Catholic. If I'd left your father, she would have disowned me. So would my dad. It simply wasn't done in those days. She put up with her husband, who drank and beat us, and she expected me to put up with mine."

"What a legacy of pain!"

"Look, I don't expect or want you to stay with Herb. But Louise, hang on to your religion."

"Sorry. Telling women to put up with awful husbands is utter paternalistic tripe, meant to keep women submissive. Especially with priests abusing little children, and the hierarchy covering up for those perverts, I frankly think the Catholic Church is the most morally bankrupt institution on the face of the earth and the greatest purveyor of misogynistic bullshit!"

Mrs. Alberts closed her eyes, as if enduring overwhelming pain. "Please do not use that language with me, Louise. I won't stand for it." She got up from her chair, collected the empty plates, and left the room.

Luli moved to the living room but she could still hear her mother sniffling in the kitchen, the dishes clattering as she put them in the dishwasher. In a few minutes, she joined her daughter on the sofa, patting her reddened nose with a tissue.

"I hope you'll reconsider about the Church."

"Mother, I don't think so. I wouldn't ask any of my children to endure a marriage like yours or mine."

"I guess you can always go to confession and come back to the Church," she sighed. "Tell me your plans now, sweetheart. Where will you live?"

"I'm moving to Santa Fe."

"Really? Why would you want to live there?"

"It's beautiful. The mountains are awe-inspiring. They change colors every hour. I'm dying to paint them. The sun shines almost every day. The light. The clarity. Shapes are sharply outlined, pine needles sparkle. Even rocks seem to glow. The skies are the most dazzling shade of turquoise," she rhapsodized. "It's a unique place. Some people even think it has a special spirituality. New Mexico has history going back thousands of years. Native Americans never lost their cultures, languages, or religion. Neither did the Spanish-speaking people, despite the influx of Anglos. Santa Fe was a thriving city before the pilgrims landed at Plymouth Rock. The arts scene is lively. I want to see if I can make it as an artist. I'm fifty now. Maybe I can finally have a life of my own."

Mrs. Alberts was incredulous. "But this is your home."

"You know, I don't think it is anymore. I don't really like Wisconsin very much. Maybe I never did, but I had nothing to compare it to. Herb's betrayal has forced me to reassess everything in my life."

"Louise, dear, we're your family—not those—those brown people, those Indians and Mexicans. Do they even speak English out there?"

"New Mexico is a state, after all. Everybody speaks English."

"How will you manage? I can give you something, but you know I don't have much money. Maybe Bart can help you."

"I'm not asking you or Bart for money. I'll find a job. Maybe I can work in a gallery. Don't worry; I'll be better off, and so will the kids."

Her mother began to weep again, large tears waterspotting the bosom of her Liz Claiborne silk dress.

11

. . . .

Luli convened a family caucus to discuss the crisis when her college-age kids came home for Jenna's graduation: Allie from Boulder, the twins from Madison. They sat in the living room around the stone hearth where the charred remains of a burnt-out fire still filled the grate.

"I'm glad he's gone," Allie said. "I hope he and his tart fall into a sinkhole full of alligators in Florida."

"Or maybe they could get stung by jellyfish?" Jenna suggested. "Some really cool poisonous ones are invading the beaches there, like the box jellyfish and physalias."

"I should have paid more attention to his business affairs," Luli said wistfully. "I wondered why he didn't want me to do his bookkeeping any more."

"Whatever you do, Mom," Jeff said. "Don't blame yourself for any of this."

"Right," Paul added. "He didn't want you to know how bad it was. I was here at Christmas when you asked how things were going with the new shopping center in De Pere, and he got pissed off, remember?" Paul imitated his father's gruff snarl: "'Everything is A-OK and butt out of my business!' Made me wonder."

"We've still got the house, though, don't we?" Allie asked.

"There's more bad news," Luli sighed. "I hired Charlie Wallborn to represent me in the divorce. He had an accountant look into Herb's finances."

"Lay it on us," Paul said. "We can take it."

"Is this gonna turn all Dickensian with debtors' prison and stuff?" Jenna asked.

"Not that bad, my darlings, but in a last ditch move to save the De Pere shopping center project from going under before construction was finished, Herb took out a huge equity loan on this house."

The kids' mouths fell open. "Can he do that without your say-so?" Paul asked. "Isn't Wisconsin a community property state?"

"That's a question Charlie has for Herb's pals at the bank. It's not the only one. How did he manage to have the house appraised for a price the accountant said was about 150% of its actual market value? And how was he able to use the money from the equity loan for his construction business?"

"Jesus H. Christ," Jeff said, shaking his head in disgust. "Crony capitalism at its finest."

"Cronies or not, your father's banker buddies are foreclosing immediately on the shopping center. It's a shame, kids, but we have to put the house up for sale."

"We don't really give a shit about this place," Paul said. "I don't want to live here anymore."

"Green Bay is such a small town," Jeff said. "After the Packers, the next favorite source of entertainment is every gory detail of other people's private lives. Somebody farts; everybody smells it. I'm sick of it."

Jenna burst into tears. "People are totally laughing at our family. How could Dad do this to us? Why wouldn't he go someplace and dry out?"

Luli hugged her youngest child. "I tried to talk him into a program many, many times—and so did his golf buddies. He has always refused to admit he has a problem."

"And he got super furious when anybody brought up the subject. I did last year, and I thought he was going to murder me," Allie said. "Fortunately, I can run a lot faster than he can."

Paul said, "Let's face it, guys. He's never going to change, and I don't want us to keep living this way, tip-toeing around him when he's drunk."

"If that's the way you feel, then it's unanimous. Let's divorce him," Luli said. "We'll survive. We're tough, and we're together. With any luck, there might be a few dollars left for your educations when the house sells. After we pay the divorce lawyer and the accountant."

"What about the cottage in Door County?" Jeff asked. "Is the bank gonna take that, too?"

Luli knew her children cared more about their vacation home than they did about the house in Green Bay. So did she. The beautifully built limestone cottage was a legacy from Luli's Norwegian great-grandfather, Lars Pettersen, who had helped settle Fish Creek in the nineteenth century.

"Every cloud has a silver lining," Luli said. "The positive side of Wisconsin's divorce laws in this case means Herb has no rights to the Fish Creek house."

"Wahoo!" the kids shrieked.

"I don't get it," Jenna said.

"The assets I owned prior to getting married belong to me. Your grandmother deeded the Pettersen real estate to your Uncle Bart and me when I was 19. Bart got the lot he built on, and I got the old cottage. My name is the only one on the deed. The attorney says Herb tried to use the property for collateral, but he couldn't get at it."

"Bastard," Jenna hissed.

"A hundred points for our team!" Paul said, giving his twin a high five.

"If the place is still ours, we could rent it out this summer," Jeff suggested.

"Dude! That is totally awesome!" Jenna said.

"What?" Luli said. "We've never done that."

"But it's a terrific idea," Allie said. "The tourist season is about to begin. Families will pay big bucks to escape the heat in Chicago or St. Louis. It's a fabulous place, stately, genteel, with room for at least a battalion."

"Yeah," Paul added. "Right on the beach, with access to the dock, and within walking distance of downtown Fish Creek. It's the coolest house ever."

"Nobody's going to be using the place this summer, any-way," Jeff said. "Unless you are, Mom. Paul and I are waiting tables at Gordon Lodge, and Uncle Bart offered us the basement apartment at his place for free. He's way pissed off at Dad."

"Jenna and I won't be in Door County, either, remember?" Allie said, "We're going to be counselors at Camp Manitowish."

"All right, let's call Jessica Burgess at her real estate firm in Fish Creek. She'll help us sort out the rental."

"There's something else, Mom," Jenna announced. "Since Herb the Turd cleaned out the college accounts, I've decided to work for a year to make money for school."

"Oh, honey, we saved since you were born so your college educations would be paid for. This breaks my heart."

"Don't fret. I'm not giving up my plans to study ocean-ography. I told Scripps I was going to do this, and they were, like, 'We'll help you find scholarships.' I've already lined up a job for this fall."

"You have?"

"Yeah. A friend of Uncle Bart's offered to hire me as a lab assistant in his med tech company in Milwaukee. He's also giving me a free apartment above their garage in exchange for babysitting."

"I am so proud of your resourcefulness. You are all really amazing," Luli said. "But what still pains me is you'll have to struggle to make it through college."

"We're gonna be fine," Allie said. "This is my last semester at CU, and it's paid for. The guys' football coach says UW alums will give them scholarships for their last two years. And we'll all help Jenna so she can go to Scripps. No problem."

"Mom," Paul reminded her. "You raised us to be strong and independent. We're not the first to have to pay for our own education. Didn't you pay for yours?"

"Yes. But my parents helped me, and then, college was affordable for middle class students. Unlike now."

Paul squeezed his mother. "Hey, we know how to hustle. Dear Old Dad taught us that."

"Fuck Dad," the other kids muttered.

"You need to clean up your language," Luli admonished her children. "After all, he is your father. You may not always feel about him as you do now."

"Forgive me, but I don't think we owe him even an ounce of respect," said Jenna. "He ruined our family."

Luli was on the verge of tears. "No, he didn't! We are still very much a family. We will always be a family. Herb's just not part of it anymore, by his own choice. It's his loss."

12

·······

Jenna's Graduation Day began with a pouring rain. The skies were leaden. Winds lashed the gangly pines surrounding the house. Wet streets, sidewalks, and driveways shone like black ice.

"Now I remember why this place depresses me," Luli said, looking out the kitchen window. She sat at the breakfast table sipping coffee with Jenna, both of them wearing wool sweaters.

"Yeah. I can't wait for California." Jenna said. "The sun, the beach, the ocean, the surfer dudes—it's gonna be awesome."

"Any news from Scripps?"

"Yes. I got an email this morning, but forgot to tell you. They think maybe I can begin second semester. An alum with a lot of bucks provides scholarships. They think I qualify."

"Fantastic."

"Mom, I totally don't want to go to graduation."

"Honey, you have worked very hard. You're graduating with honors, after all."

"Whatever."

"C'mon, this is cause for celebration. Why do you think we're all still here? And your grandmother—she is so proud of you. We all are."

Luli thought the graduation ceremony dragged on far too long, but then they always did. Jenna was as gloomy as the Green Bay skies, in spite of graduating near the top of her class, and earning a National Honor Society mention for her good grades. She wasn't in the mood to go to her graduation party. Instead, Grandmother Alberts invited the family to everyone's favorite restaurant, the Union Hotel in De Pere. The maître d' showed them to a private dining room upstairs in one of the former hotel rooms.

"I love this place," Grandmother Alberts said when they sat down. "It's over a hundred and twenty years old. Our family could only afford to eat here once in a great while."

Luli started to say this is where she and Herb had their wedding reception, and her brothers had often fetched their father home dead drunk from the Union's bar. But, she decided, some aspects of family history were best left alone.

"Dad Brashier used to live here," Mrs. Alberts said.

"Who's he, Grandma?" Jenna asked.

"Why, he was the Packers' equipment manager for years. A friend of your grandfather's. A legendary figure."

"He's the guy who came up with the "G" symbol, right, Mother?" Luli said.

"That's what people say."

"Cool!" the Russell children said almost in unison.

"What are you going to have, Mother?" Luli asked.

"The lamb chops, of course. Order whatever you want. This is my treat." She reached over and kissed Jenna, on her right, and extended a hand across the table to Allie. "We're celebrating you, Allie, as well. You girls' graduations are extremely special to me. All those honors. And you, Allie, with three degrees now. I never even graduated from high school. You're making me burst the buttons on my brand new Oscar de la Renta dress!"

"It's very pretty, Grandma," Allie said. "Rose is a good color for you."

"Rose is a good color for most people. This was on sale at the shop. I was so worried it would sell before I could buy it."

Over dessert—the restaurant's famous strawberry schaum torte—Luli gave her daughters the gifts she'd bought them in New Mexico. "These are traditional necklaces from Santo Domingo Pueblo, south of Santa Fe. The birds are hand carved turquoise, obsidian, bone, and melon shell."

Allie put her necklace on and grinned. "I love it. Thanks!"

"Sweet! Thank you, Mom," Jenna said, and burst into tears.

After Allie flew back to Boulder to defend her thesis, they held a huge garage sale and gave away the remaining household goods nobody wanted. Luli packed up Mrs. Phlegmish with her art supplies and her favorite clothes, photographs, books, and paintings. The kids left for their summer jobs, and a "For Sale" sign went up in front of their house.

Mrs. Alberts came to say goodbye. She and Luli stood in the driveway beside the car. "I wish you wouldn't leave, Louise. Are you sure this is what's best for you?"

"This is absolutely what I want. A fresh start in a new place." Luli wrapped her arms around her mother and kissed her cheek. "I'm not abandoning you. You can come visit me in Santa Fe!"

"You know I hate to travel," Mrs. Alberts sniffled. "I have no intention of ever getting on an airplane."

"You can take a train from Milwaukee to Chicago, and from there, it's Amtrak to Albuquerque."

"Hmmmmph," Mrs. Alberts replied.

While Luli drove to Boulder for Allie's graduation, she listened to Books on Tape and NPR to keep her mind occupied. She arrived at her daughter's apartment near the University late in the afternoon of the second day.

"You made it here in a day and a half, Mom. You must be exhausted," Allie said.

"Not really, dear. Actually, I'm feeling pretty upbeat. The start of a new life!"

"Yeah, I've been thinking about that. All of us are going down new paths—you, me, Jenna, the boys. Even Dad."

Luli let out a deep breath. "He's not my problem anymore. Maybe one day you kids will want a relationship with him, but for me he's history."

"I don't care if I ever see that bastard again."

After dinner at a neighborhood brewpub, Luli was ready to sleep. "See what happens when you combine a long drive, high altitude, and really good beer?" Allie said. "You take the bed. I'll sleep on the sofa."

Luli began to protest, but her daughter insisted. They lay in the dark talking.

"I'm sure each of you has had bad moments, but I'm so proud of how well you've all handled a difficult situation. You're truly adults now. Which makes me both sad and happy."

"I get the happy part, but why sad? Explain."

"Well, I can't help being nostalgic. There were times when things were good for us as a family, especially when you were little. You were all beautiful, healthy babies, then funny, smart toddlers I couldn't keep up with. I mean, you absolutely bowled me over when you asked me what infinity meant."

"How old was I? Twenty-five?"

"No, three! Herb didn't believe me when I told him. He didn't drink as much then," Luli said wistfully. "And he made time to play with you, to be a real father when you were little."

"What happened?"

"I think he started to go downhill when he realized he wasn't making as much money as he thought he should, and he probably never would. It depressed him that he didn't have the wealth or expensive toys his friends had. I told him

I didn't care about any of that. But he did. I offered to go back to teaching when Jenna started middle school. But he didn't want me to work. Said it made him look bad. Like he couldn't afford to support us."

"Ugh. That's pathetic."

"It's still like that in Green Bay. Career women are a rarity. How many of your friends' mothers had jobs?"

"Only Marguerite's. She started teaching French again after her husband was diagnosed with MS."

"Right. Working women are mostly poor, single, or widowed. Maybe some wives are happy enough staying home—but I'm ready to start a new life. It occurs to me that I've never really been on my own."

"You'll do great. Getting out of Wisconsin is certainly a move in the right direction."

Luli's grin was so bright it almost glowed in the dark.

"It's all your fault I hit the road."

"Really?"

"Well, you and your sibs'. It was your idea to send me to Santa Fe. You found me a place to stay, you got me paints and painting lessons. And you probably knew instinctively that your father wouldn't show up. You enabled me to discover that a new world was possible. Maybe I could become a painter after all, live someplace more interesting, meet new people. Without your gift, I might never have considered doing something different."

"Mom, I have to confess something. I feel like Jenna did. I don't want to go to my graduation either."

"Allie! A Ph.D. is a major accomplishment. You're the first woman in our family to earn a doctorate. This is huge. I'm sorry I'm the only one who can be here, but you know we're all very, very proud of you. You're graduating magna cum laude!"

"'With great praise,' huh. Cool. At least those three years of high school Latin are good for something.

"Mom, with all of us scattering to different places, promise me we're still a family."

"Absolutely! Of course we are. The nest has unraveled, but our life in it hasn't been good for a long time—not for me, not for you, or your sibs—maybe not even for your father."

"Like I give a shit about him."

Luli took in a deep breath and exhaled slowly. "No matter how many miles apart we are, we'll still be together. Your father may not be part of our lives. But we don't need him. We will always have each other, sweetheart."

Luli helped Allie empty out her apartment and ship a few boxes to Wisconsin to store in Grandmother Alberts' garage. On the long day's drive south to Santa Fe, they passed the time talking.

"Have you decided what's next, Allie?"

"After Camp Manitowish I want to find a job, save some money, do a little traveling. Craig's going to law school at the University of Chicago. We're planning to live together. I hope you won't be wigged out about it."

"Honey, he's a terrific guy. You know I like him. You seem happy together. Ten years ago, the thought my daughter would be shacking up might have upset me, but not anymore. Please don't be in a hurry to marry. See how it goes sharing an apartment. Believe me, it's not easy. Don't take this the wrong way. I am so grateful to have you, but, don't make the mistake I made and end up pregnant."

"Not to worry. I am absolutely not ready for motherhood."

Allie stayed in Santa Fe for a few days seeing the sights.

"This is a fab place, Mom. I can see why you love it here. For a town that's not very big, it's surprisingly sophisticated. It has history. I love the architecture. The Farmers' Market is delightful and the wonderful little Mexican restaurants you've taken me to—I could eat 'til I burst."

"Santa Fe knows good food. I'll have to watch my waistline."

"It's also a walking town. If you keep pounding the pavement in your size eights, the tacos won't stick to your hips. I'm sorry I didn't get to meet the Alires, though."

"Next time. Their neighbor says they're up north fishing. They truly are the most amazing family. I don't think I could have gotten through this without them."

"Santa Fe really is beautiful. I can't wait to see how your painting evolves."

"I'm so taken with the sky, especially the clouds. Everyday it's a new display of shapes, colors, movement. I've never seen two days look the same. Even the mountains are ever changing, depending on the light. Some days they're dark and brooding, other days they sparkle, especially after a rain."

"Sounds like you're on your way, Mom. Brava!"

13

· · · · · · ·

THE MORNING AFTER ALLIE LEFT, LULI WAS WALKING along Washington Avenue on her way to buy a newspaper at La Fonda when she saw Adán deadheading flowers and plucking cigarette butts out of the Hotel Plaza Real's planters. She crossed the street and tapped him on the shoulder.

Adán smiled broadly, swept off his bill cap, and shook her hand.

"You're back in town. How was the fishing?"

"We caught a dozen trout. In fact, the grandkids caught most of them. Rosealba and I have been wondering when we'd see you." He mopped the sweat off his brow with his bandana. "I'm sorry we didn't answer your letter. We're not much for writing."

She shrugged. "Don't worry. I wasn't expecting a reply. I just wanted you to know I was thinking about you and planning to come back."

"Is everything working out?" Adán asked.

"Well, yes and no. I mean, the divorce is almost a done deal. The kids are fine with it, and as traumatic as it has been, I think it's best for everybody."

Adán nodded. "We have an idea about where you can live. Why don't you come for dinner on Sunday, and we can talk about it. Besides," he grinned, "there's somebody who's been wanting to meet you."

"Basura?"

He laughed. "Sure. But I mean somebody else besides him."

"How mysterious." He probably meant a member of his huge extended family, but she didn't know why any of them would be interested in her.

"Rosealba usually has Sunday dinner around one. Is that all right?"

"Perfect. Tell her I'll bring dessert."

Since there were no kitchen facilities in her temporary quarters at the Thunderbird Motel, Luli decided to buy a triple-whammy chocolate cake from the Chocolate Maven. It was an extravagance, but for the Alires, whose generosity had been extraordinary, she could afford it. Their comfort, solace, and hours of patient listening before she returned to Wisconsin saved her sanity.

The Ford lumbered to the top of the rutted dirt road early Sunday afternoon. A mop of orange and brown fur flew over the adobe wall and hurled itself at Luli's tires, lunging at them, growling and snapping. When she got out, Basura raced around the station wagon to bark a welcome. "Help!" she laughed. "Save me from this ferocious dog."

Rosealba emerged from the house in her ever-present apron. She and Luli hugged while the dog vied for attention. "¡Calma, Basura!" Rosealba scolded. "Settle down."

Ignoring his mistress, the dog leaped high in the air, nipping at Luli's hand until she scratched his ears. She reached into the car, took a bakery box off the passenger seat, and gave it to Rosealba. As soon as he caught sight of the box, Basura sat on his heels, batting his big brown eyes.

"Not in your wildest dreams, Basura," Rosealba laughed as she clutched the box and squeezed Luli's shoulders gently with her free arm. "It's so good to have you back. We think about you lots."

Luli followed Rosealba through the house to the backyard where she immediately saw the apricot tree was densely dotted with little bright green globes. "You were right," she exclaimed. "It's an apricot year."

"Told you," Rosealba said cheerfully. "Soon as they're ripe let's make jam. It's much easier canning with other people, and we'll have fun."

"Yeah—a jam session."

Rosealba gave Luli a blank look.

"A jam session—like when musicians get together to play music."

"Oh, I see. In fact, my daughter Beatriz wants to help. It's high time you met her."

"You're on."

Rosealba led Luli to a vine-covered arbor on the west side of the yard overlooking the city. Adán stood up to shake Luli's hand. A frail, elderly man also got up from his chair, holding onto the tabletop with both hands to support himself. The breeze lifted strands of his sparse white hair from a broad forehead freckled with liver spots and red splotches. Milky blue-gray eyes took Luli in. He grasped her hand with a quick feeble grip.

"Van Buren Phillips," he said in a thin voice.

Seeing his unsteadiness, Luli instantly sat down, and everyone else followed suit. For a minute while no one said anything, the elderly man looked expectantly from Adán to Luli then back to Adán.

Finally, Adán spoke. "I guess you don't recognize Mr. Phillips, Luli."

"Flip," he interjected. "Just call me Flip," he said, looking down the baggy legs of his frayed khakis to the worn white canvas Top-Siders a few sizes too big for his feet.

Luli studied him. His bony face laced with blue veins at the temples. The red, gnarled bulb at the end of his otherwise fine-ridged nose. The threadbare navy blue blazer that hung on him as if his stooped shoulders were a wire hanger. The basketball-sized round belly pushing against his thin white shirt.

"Oh my God," she said, realizing who he was.

Adán and Flip exchanged a wry grin.

"You're OK," she said, then corrected herself. "I mean . . . I didn't think . . . I mean . . ."

Flip lifted a hand from the chair arm. "Please, Mrs. Russell. You would be entirely correct in assuming that I did not survive this spring's unfortunate incident. Indeed, were it not for you and Mr. Alire, and your timely intervention, I would surely have succumbed to the ravages of my illness. I very much appreciate your thoughtfulness in seeing me to the hospital. It was most kind and generous of you to concern yourself with my welfare. I should like to take this opportunity to express my gratitude to you both. I shall search for a way to repay your kindness."

Flip told Luli that shortly after his admission to the hospital, Adán had begun to visit him, sometimes alone, sometimes with Rosealba.

"The Alires are amazingly well-connected at St. Vincent's," Flip said. "Indeed, I think they're related to half the staff. Their relatives—nurses, orderlies, volunteers—were instrumental in seeing that I received excellent attention. I was particularly taken with a delightful young woman internist, Dr. Inés Pacheco, who's a niece, I believe."

Adán smiled. "She's my cousin's daughter. We're all so proud of her."

"And so you should be," Flip said. "She appears to be an outstanding clinician, with a marvelous bedside manner."

As the old gentleman raved about the care he had received at the hospital, his formality and demeanor struck Luli as almost British. It was clear Flip Phillips was no garden-variety street bum.

Rosealba set a tray laden with tall glasses of watermelon juice down on the table, passed one to each guest, and sat beside her husband. As they ate roast chicken and calabacitas, Luli learned that since his release from the hospital, Flip had been living in the Alires' guesthouse, recently vacated by their youngest son Arturo when he moved to Albuquerque to attend UNM. Flip described the arrangement as a "temporary situation." When he indicated some embarrassment at being dependent upon the Alires for his room and board, Rosealba leaned over and put her hand gently on his.

"Flip, we're happy to have you here. This place is too empty with all our kids gone. I don't know how to cook for just two of us, you know. You're saving my poor husband from a steady diet of leftovers."

Noting the minuscule amount of food Flip consumed, Luli knew Rosealba was exaggerating to make him feel welcome.

During dessert—Luli's chocolate cake and coffee—the Alires told her about a housesitting situation, an immediate solution to her housing problem, at least for the time being. One of their neighbors on Alire Circle, as the hilltop neighborhood was called, was a well-known writer who was going to be in France for at least a year working on a new book.

"When he asked us if we could take care of his house and garden for him during his absence, we instantly thought of you," Adán said, "knowing you needed a place to live. The neighbor said if you pay the utilities, look after his beloved roses, and keep the house in good order, the place is yours until he comes home next summer."

Luli was ecstatic. "We're going to be neighbors. This is perfect. I promise to kiss your neighbor's roses every day and keep his home spotless. I have been so concerned about where I was going to live. I know rents are really high here. Now all I have to do is find a job and decide what I'm going to do with the rest of my life."

"I have a job," Flip announced in his small, tremulous voice.

Everyone looked at him in surprise.

"You do?" Rosealba said.

Flip smiled. "Yes. I begin tomorrow morning with the sun. Think of it—the initiation of a new career at my age." He seemed quite pleased with himself.

"Oh? What sort of job, Flip?" Adán asked.

"In the field of communications, marketing and distribution," he continued, a twinkle in his faded eyes. Seeing the Alires exchange anxious looks, Flip grinned broadly and his eyes gleamed. He moved closer and patted Rosealba's hand. "I believe you would probably refer to my position as that of a newspaper vendor. Corner of Alameda and Don Gaspar. Quite a prime location. I must have wowed them at the interview."

Everyone laughed.

"Are you sure you're up to it, Flip?" Rosealba asked. "You know, that means being outside all day, even if that corner is one of the shadiest spots in town."

The old man shrugged. "We'll see how it goes."

14

· · · · · · ·

Luli moved into the Alire Circle house the next day with her few belongings. She settled her clothing into the closet and the dresser the writer had cleared out before decamping for France, then she wrote each of her children to tell them where she was.

"The Alires found me a fabulous housesitting job right next door to them. It's a true Santa Fe adobe on a hilltop with a million-dollar view of the city, and the best part is, it's free. It's mine for a year. I hope you can come visit me soon. There's plenty of room. I miss all of you terribly."

Luli picked the sunniest spot in the house by a south-facing window and set up her studio. She covered a table with oilcloth and organized her supplies in a set of Tarahumara baskets from Jackalope. She placed her clean brushes on a dragon-shaped antique sumi brush rest she'd found at a yard sale in Green Bay for five dollars. A buffet table in the dining room with shallow drawers was perfect for paper storage and finished work. Loren's going-away present, an elegant leather portfolio, fit neatly into the hall closet. Once she had found a place for everything, she stood admiring her new workspace. Best of all, it was *her* studio, warm and sunny, not cold and dank, with no one else's priorities in the way.

The following morning, Luli put several of her best paintings into the portfolio and set forth to visit Canyon Road, a street famous for its galleries. "Maybe one of them will take me on as an employee, or maybe even as an artist," she thought.

At her first stop, while she waited for the woman behind the desk to finish her telephone call, Luli checked out the paintings. Most of them were of howling coyotes in flat, kindergarten colors—bright red, royal blue—with bandannas around their necks, set in orange and purple landscapes. Finally, the woman hung up.

"May I help you?" she asked in a smoky voice, examining her fingernails without making eye contact with Luli.

"Uh, I'm looking for a gallery to represent my work. May I show you some of my watercolors?"

The woman laughed. "We only handle the owners' paintings, dear. And that's me."

At the next gallery, featuring messy abstracts, nobody appeared for several minutes. Finally, a man emerged from the back room pulling up the zipper up on his jeans. He brushed his stringy hair from his high forehead and stared at Luli standing in the middle of the gallery. "Yeah?" he said curtly. He noticed her portfolio and waved her off. "We've got more artists than we need, doll. What we need are customers."

She visited ten more galleries. Most of the people were indifferent and dismissive. A few were friendly. Finally one woman about Luli's age offered her a chair and a cup of tea.

"Are you new at this game?" she asked.

"Yes. A gallery at home represented my work, but I've moved here now, and I'm trying to find my niche."

"Let's see what you've got. I'm Savannah, and you're . . ."

"Luli. I'm pleased to meet you." She untied the string on her portfolio and passed it to Savannah, who leafed through the unframed paintings.

"These are lovely, a hint of Monet, a touch of Cézanne— if either had painted the Midwest, that is. Where are you from?"

"Green Bay. Wisconsin."

Savannah nodded. "Certainly these are appropriate for that part of the country—the stylized birches, the mossy limestone cliffs, the choppy lakes, smoky skies. I'm sure you've had some success."

"Yes, my gallery has sold a number of my paintings—to banks, corporations, collectors."

Savannah looked at Luli over her half-frame glasses. "I'm going to give it to you straight. You're a good painter, but these are not Santa Fe. Our customers come here from New York, California, even Switzerland, Japan, France. They're looking for artwork that reminds them of this place—the mountains, the sunsets, the dramatic panoramas . . ."

"And the red coyotes?"

Savannah laughed. "Ah, yes. You've been to Meredith Federman's, haven't you?"

Luli nodded.

"You don't have to go quite as far as she does with the so-called Santa Fe style. But you need to paint what's here, your interpretation of New Mexico. That's what we can sell. Blame it on Georgia O'Keeffe," she shrugged.

"Here's my card. Settle in. Then paint! When you've got something to show us—at least five or six paintings you're proud of—make an appointment to see either Jules, the owner, or me. Don't come in with the actual paintings, though. Such a no-no. Show us professional photos of your work, a CD, or a PowerPoint presentation. Can you do that?"

"Sure," Luli said, having no idea what a power point was. "Thank you so much for your help. You've been more than kind."

Savannah smiled. "I'm from Minneapolis myself. I've been here ten years. Santa Fe's a wonderful town. I love it. But it's tough to break into the art scene, believe me. I'm lucky if I sell ten postcards of my work a month—and maybe a painting or two a year. Good luck, Luli."

Figuring stores would be open around eleven, Luli pulled up her sagging panty hose, gave her Aerosole flats another swipe of the polishing cloth, and tugged her skirt down over her hips. She clutched sheaves of the résumé her kids had helped her put together in a midnight session before they all left Green Bay, and stepped out into what she hoped would be the World of Work.

Luli hadn't held a job—a salaried job, anyway—for twenty years. Even then, she had only worked as a substitute second grade teacher for four years in a Catholic school where she didn't need a teaching certificate. She quit when she got pregnant with the twins and hadn't worked outside her home since then. Unless you counted the bookkeeping she'd done for Herb's business until he shut her out.

A red sun was slipping toward the purple horizon on the far side of Santa Fe when Luli returned home. She parked Mrs. Phlegmish by the adobe wall alongside her house, let herself in, and collapsed on the living room sofa. For hours, she lay staring up at the dark vigas in the white ceiling, examining every knot hole and adze mark in the ancient beams holding up the sagging flat roof.

She was too dazed to cry.

The sort of employment she thought would be easy to land—a sales position in a gallery—was not to be had. The few places looking for help wanted someone with computer skills, a person with special knowledge of Indian arts, historic Southwestern painters, local contemporary artists. Even if she had the qualifications the galleries were looking for—and she didn't—the work was part-time, there were no benefits, and starting pay was barely above minimum wage.

The next day, summoning her courage once again, she set out for the Plaza. After a number of unsuccessful inquiries, she called on an imports store on San Francisco Street with a "Help Wanted" sign in the window. The owner, a stoop-shouldered man with a bad comb over, clutched her arm, brushing her breast with his hand "accidentally."

"Let's go into my office." His eyes cruising up and down her body, he practically dragged her to the back of the store, closed the door behind them, and led her to a seat.

Leaning above her, gripping the arms of the chair, he spoke inches from her face. "You're looking for a job, sugar?" he said in his clumsy attempt at a croon.

To avoid his overwhelming cigarette breath, Luli drew away from him as far as possible without tipping her chair over backward.

"So what are your qualifications?" he asked in a croaky voice, stroking her gold necklace and eyeing her breasts. "How about a kiss," he said. Luli swung her purse at him and stomped out of his office.

The old lecher cackled, calling out after her as she sped angrily out of his junk palace. "You're not gonna find anything in this town, sweetheart. You housewife types are a dime a dozen."

Doing her best to keep going, Luli walked the rest of the entire downtown area, entering any business that looked promising, trying to talk to whoever seemed to be in charge, and leaving her résumé. As she did her best to smile and be upbeat, the horrible man's words echoed in her ears, a mantra of scorn drumming in her head as her feet pounded the pock-marked pavement of Santa Fe's sidewalks. What angered her the most was she knew he was right.

Home in her borrowed adobe, Luli curled up on the sofa, biting her nails, and sifting through her options as a lemon-tinged twilight filtered through the slats of the wooden blinds. If she went back to Green Bay, somebody—from the country club, her former church, a neighbor—would take pity on her and give her a job as a secretary or a file clerk. They'd make allowances for her not having any relevant experience and not being able to type very well. Nobody in Santa Fe would. But the idea of doing that, especially returning in defeat, nauseated her.

No sooner had this awful thought crossed her mind than someone knocked gently. She combed her fingers through her hair, smoothed her mussed clothes, and padded to the entryway in her sore, stocking feet. She saw Rosealba carrying a pie plate covered with a dishtowel and opened the screen for her.

"Here's some tamale pie for you. Hope you like it. How did your job-hunting go today?"

Luli smiled, but give-away tears leaked out the corners of her eyes. Without waiting for an answer, Rosealba set the dish on the hall table, led her to the couch, and sat down, her leathery hands holding Luli's soft ones.

"Oooh, I'm sorry. It's tough, isn't it? But you'll find something, Dios mediante. God provides. You just started looking."

"I don't know if I can do this again. It was awful. Demeaning. Nobody would give me the time of day. A lady in one gallery took the résumé I had given her and as I was leaving, out of the corner of my eye, I saw her toss it in the trash—practically right under my nose." The tears flowed down her cheeks, dripping from her chin onto her blouse like rivulets off a roof.

Rosealba took a handkerchief out of her apron pocket and dried Luli's wet cheeks. "Ay, m'ija, it's not that bad..."

Luli sniffled. "Oh, yes it is. I'm down to my last five hundred bucks, Rosie. The car's acting strange and slipping gears, like maybe there's a problem with the transmission. Herb maxed out all the credit cards and they were in his name, so I don't even have that to fall back on. I can't ask my mother or brother or any of my friends for money. I've never been in a situation like this before. I don't know what I'm going to do."

Rosealba patted her arm. "Something will turn up for you. I know it will. You're not experienced in this town yet. Look, I brought you this morning's *New Mexican*. It will help you find places where they want somebody. You can't go into every tienda in town trying to get hired, m'ija. Here, you keep this."

After Rosealba left, Luli picked up the paper and turned to the Classifieds. Surely there were jobs in hotels or restaurants. The kind of minimum wage gigs the twins and their friends bounced in and out of like jumping frogs—reception clerk, restaurant hostess, cashier, hotel maid. She knew she wouldn't qualify as a waitress or a cook. With her cash rapidly dwindling, she needed to find something without delay, even if the pay was peanuts.

The "Miscellaneous Employment" column listed a number of jobs that appeared to be carefully disguised positions for telephone solicitors. "Start immediately! Training provided!" Luli hated getting those calls, invariably, the second she put dinner on the table. "I'll dig ditches before I become one of those awful people," she murmured to herself.

Other job listings were inappropriate. What was CDL truck driving? "Training in four weeks! Financing available!"

There were a few advertisements for sales openings, but what did Luli know about car parts? Irrigation equipment? Tractors? Further down the column, a small announcement caught her eye: "Art Restoration Studio looking for part-time help. Sales experience, bookkeeping skills, and Spanish fluency helpful."

"Hmmmm," Luli thought. "Sales? Well, I was quite successful at selling Girl Scout cookies and raffle tickets for my kids' school fundraisers. I'm somewhat qualified as a bookkeeper, although my computer skills aren't very good.

Spanish? I aced it in high school. I'll buy a book and study fast. Maybe I'll remember more than I think."

The ad didn't provide a telephone number, but it listed a street address on Old Santa Fe Trail. Rosealba told her it wasn't far away.

"You can walk there, hija. It's maybe twenty minutes. I'll save the newspaper for you tomorrow. But ¿quién sabe? Maybe this is your new job."

15

. . . .

RELUCTANT TO FACE ANOTHER DISAPPOINTING search, Luli lingered in bed the following morning. She breakfasted on toast and a pot of tea, dressed in a simple paisley dress, put on make up, polished her shoes, and went out again, her folder of résumés tucked under her arm, her back straight, her walk confident.

The one-story adobe wasn't far from the State Capitol on a narrow street that had been the end of the historic Santa Fe Trail. A rusted iron sign read "Antiques." The door was ajar. She pushed it open and walked into an unlit room jumbled with antique pottery, wood furniture, candle-sticks. Weavings were draped over a few worn upholstered chairs. She could hear men talking and laughing in another room.

"Hello?" No answer. "Hello?" she called again, this time louder. The talking stopped. A pudgy, pleasant-looking man in his fifties entered the room, wiping his hands on a rag. A cigarette dangled from a corner of his mouth. "Yes?" he said, squinting from the smoke curling upward into his eyes as he gave her an approving appraisal, looking her up and down.

Luli took a deep breath, bracing herself for some stupid, sexist remark. "Hi, I'm Luli Russell. I'm here in response to the ad you put in the newspaper looking for sales help," she said cheerfully.

The man balanced the cigarette on the edge of a table, and shook her hand amiably. "Yes, I am look for a help with this . . ." his glance swept the room, "this disastre of a shop. I am Alberto Colilla. Tell me again your name . . . ?"

"I'm Luli . . . Mrs. Luli Russell."

"You are married?"

Luli decided to lie in case this guy was a sleazeball groper like the old bastard downtown.

"Uh, yes. What do you need me to do?"

"Everything," Alberto said. His arms flying, encompassing the entire room, he ticked off duties. "You wait on the customers, but we don't have so many. You make the sales. Maybe you clean up some, oil the furnitures. You make the shop look nicer. A woman's touch. I'm not so good with the peoples. I work on broken stuff in my workshop. When somebody come for their things I fix, you take the money, you write them a receipt."

He picked up his cigarette, drew on it, and exhaled a long stream of smoke into the air above Luli's head. "¿Hablas español?"

She shrugged. "I studied it in high school, and I understand some. But I'm not really fluent. I'd like to learn, though." She hoped she didn't sound too eager. "How much is the pay, Mr. . . . ."

"Colilla. But you call me Beto. How about $10 the hour?"

"Well . . ." She was ready to take his offer, but then Beto said: "Bueno, $11. Is good to start?"

"Sure. Do you want to see my résumé?"

He waved away the papers she held out to him. "It don't make a difference. I know you can do this work. We have a deal?"

"Si, señor," Luli smiled.

Beto showed her around the gallery space. He pointed out a number of items, told her where they were from, the ages, the values. Nothing had a price tag. Some things seemed cheap, others were very dear. Luli was overwhelmed. "I . . . I don't know if I can remember all this," she said.

"Just say no to worry. I am work in the back. You have a question, you ask me. I give you books to read. Come. I introduce you to my friends in the workshop. They are mostly chilenos like me, artists from Chile. They carve the wood, they make the frames, they clean the paintings. They keep me company while I work."

Luli followed Beto into the smoky, low-ceilinged back room. Four men who were lounging on chairs got up when she walked into the cramped space. Like Beto, they gave her a stem-to-stern evalutation, lingering on the important parts, as if she were a racehorse up for sale. But their smiles were friendly, and they were polite. One offered her his chair, but she stayed standing. As Beto introduced the men, each came forward to shake her hand. They were all in need of a shave, with smoke-stained teeth, and large, mournful, deep brown eyes. Except for the younger man whose head was thick with loose curls, they all had straight black hair like Beto's, combed back from their foreheads and kept in place with some sort of pomade in a style Luli associated with swells of the 1920s and '30s. They wore dark clothes, thrift store sports coats with faded jeans and boots. The youngest, Kiko, wore a black T-shirt advertising a Goth band that the boys and Jenna would probably recognize, but she didn't.

Luli noticed a white carved wood figure on the workbench. "Is this something you're working on, Beto?"

"Yes. Is a katsina. Or, it will be a katsina."

"I don't know what that is."

"A doll, from the Hopi Indians. For the ceremonies. Kiko, he carve it from the cottonwood root. I show him how. Next I paint it. Then I bang it up a little and put it on the roof for a month."

The men laughed and murmured among themselves in Spanish. Luli was puzzled, but decided not to ask questions.

Ché accepted a gourd cup from the man beside him and sipped something through a silver straw. Then he offered it to Luli. "Is yerba mate, from my country, Argentina," he said.

"Try it, Luli. Is good and gives energy," Beto said. Noting her hesitancy, he took a clean straw from a can by the sink. "This is the bombilla. Is a metal straw for drink the mate. The English, they use a tea bag or a strainer to keep out the tea leaves. With the bombilla, no leaves; they stay in the cup."

Luli took the straw and examined a miniature sieve at its bottom. "Clever," she said. She took a sip. "Hmmm. Sort of like green tea. A little bitter—interesting."

"You want, I can make you a cup," said Beto.

"Thank you. I drank quite a lot of tea at home this morning. Another day." She smiled and gave the gourd back.

"Is a social thing," Ché said. "I introduce to these chilenos. Now we drink mate all the time."

"When you can start?" Beto asked.

"Tomorrow?" she said hopefully.

"Sure. I am here by ten." He shook her hand, as did each of the men in turn. "Hasta mañana."

"¡Hasta mañana!" Luli replied, proud of herself for answering in Spanish.

To celebrate her new job, she invited the Alires and Flip for dinner, serving them meatloaf and scalloped potatoes, a green salad, and for dessert, an apple pie she bought at Kaune's. Flip barely ate anything, but revived when he saw the pie.

"And you serve it with cheddar cheese," he said. "Good girl."

Luli could see the Alires were surprised by the combination. "It's a Wisconsin tradition," she explained. "You don't have to try it." But they both did.

"Oooh, ¡sabroso!" Rosealba said. "It's like when you eat membrillo with a sharp cheese like manchego. You're a wonderful cook."

"This is one of the few meals I can make with my eyes closed."

Adán wanted to know about her new boss.

Rosealba laughed. "I told Danny about that awful man in the store downtown who . . . who didn't respect you when you interviewed for a job. He's being protective, like he was of our girls. He wants to make sure this man is a gentleman."

"He's from Chile, in South America, but he has been here many years. He restores antiques and sells them, repairs old paintings, cleans them. His artist friends help out."

"I'll ask around town about him," Adán said. "What's his name?"

On her days off and some evenings, Luli visited Flip in his tiny house. She noticed a large book on the end table by his armchair, and bent down to read the title. "*Flannery O'Connor: The Complete Stories*. She's one of my favorites."

"Mine, too. I found this at Open Hands. A bargain at twenty-five cents, but I regret to say, I can't lift it. It weighs a ton."

"Would you like me to read it to you?"

"Why, yes, if you have the energy to hold up such a tome." Flip's eyes brightened.

Luli enjoyed reading to Flip, and he loved being read to. In addition to the O'Connor stories, she read to him from newspapers and magazines. His favorites were the daily news from *The New York Times* or *The Wall Street Journal*, articles from *The New Yorker*, and short stories. He'd lie comfortably in the armchair, his feet propped on the hassock, his eyes closed as he listened. If he felt up to it, they'd talk about what she had read.

"You read very well, my dear," he told her.

"Thanks, Flip. Books have saved my life. When I was growing up, reading was my way of escaping . . . unpleasantness in our house. In summer, I'd read in the tree house my brother Nat built for me. In cold weather, I'd go hide in my room, close the door, put in earplugs, and read."

"Earplugs?"

"Well, my father was . . . he was a heavy drinker. He and my mother fought a lot. I couldn't stand to hear their battles."

Flip nodded. "Yes, we drinkers are a burdensome lot," he murmured, and quickly changed the subject. "What do you like to read?"

"Everything. As a kid, I especially liked biographies. There was a series, bound in orange. I think I read them all—Florence Nightingale, Thomas Edison, Betsy Ross, Babe Ruth, Kit Carson . . ."

"I'll bet they didn't tell the whole story about Kit Carson."

Luli smiled. "No, probably not. Later, I enjoyed novels set in exotic locales—especially those by Isak Dinesen, Hemingway, Graham Greene, Kipling, Pearl Buck. I've always wanted to travel in the worst way."

"And have you?"

Luli shook her head sadly. "No, I've never been anywhere. Not even to Canada. But maybe someday."

"You'll travel. Now you're on your own, I foresee a whole new world will open up for you."

"Well, but travel takes money, and Herb left us without a dime."

Flip winked. "Ah, but who knows what the morrow brings?"

At the Santa Fe Library, Luli checked out books for Flip to read on his own. It was housed in a former police station downtown within easy walking distance of her house. The staff helped her choose slim, lightweight volumes Flip could hold in his palsied hands. They also showed her how to use their free computers. In no time she became a library regular.

Except for the ever-present pall of cigarette smoke that floated out of the back room, the job at Beto's was good enough.

"To start, maybe you clean and try to make order in this room," he suggested her first day.

Everything was coated in a thick layer of dust. The wood plank floor was filthy, the merchandise was jumbled and disorganized. Pottery and sculptures were tipped over; paintings leaned against the walls or were stacked up on the floor. The glass display cases were so dirty she couldn't see what was in them. She cleaned as best she could. Beto came out of his studio from time to time to see how she was doing or help her move large pieces of furniture. He'd use the visits to explain his gallery's specialty.

"Spanish Colonial means from the time of the Spanish conquest in the late 1400s to about 1820, when América Latina win her independence from Spain. Some works also show the Moor influence, the Italian, the Philippine, the indigenous. Even the Portuguese and Dutch, especially the ones from Brazil." He pointed out a two-foot high dark wood niche with a scrolled pediment and matching carving on the edges of its two doors. "Is an ofertôrio. From the northeast of Brazil. You have your saint in it, maybe some flowers. Is like an altar for the home."

Luli nodded as if she understood what Beto told her, even when she was clueless.

16

· · · · · · ·

"LULI, IT'S TIME FOR OUR JAM SESSION," ROSEALBA announced in late July. "The apricots are ready. We can't let them get mushy. If they fall on the ground it's a fiesta for the ants. Are you free this weekend?"

"The gallery has been quiet lately. I'm sure Beto won't mind if I take Saturday off. I used to help my mother can, but that was a long time ago. What do we need?"

"Let's see . . . sugar, lemons, maybe some of that almond liquor. Oh, and pectin, to thicken the jam. Then you don't need so much sugar."

"I'll buy all this at Albertson's. Should I get some Mason jars?"

"We have enough. I make the people I give jam to give me back the jars and bands later, but we'll need new lids. I'll put them on the list."

The extended Alire family, including Luli and Flip, picked apricots after work all week. They stored them in buckets and boxes in a shed beside the house. Saturday morning dawned cool and unusually cloudy.

"Maybe it will rain," Rosealba said hopefully. "Canning's not much fun when it's too hot in your kitchen. In fact, we're going to cook the jam outside on the gas grill, under the porch roof. Adán's got it all cleaned up and ready to go."

While Rosealba washed out glass jars, bands, and lids and sterilized them, Daniel and his little brother, Renzo, Luli, and Adán tossed aside blemished fruit, washed the apricots, halved them, took out the dark brown pits, and dropped the halves into stew pots.

Rosealba noticed the boys were eating almost as many as they were splitting open.

"Save some for the jam," she laughed. "Besides, too many of them fruits might give you a tummy ache."

They heard a motorcycle roar up the driveway and stop by the house. An exuberant young woman in jeans and a denim shirt bounced into the kitchen, followed by a tall man with a heavy black beard. Rosealba wiped her hands on her apron and enveloped the woman in her arms.

"This is my Beatriz, Luli. And this guy, Mr. Barbudo, is Joe, her fiancé."

Both shook Luli's hand. Joe hugged Rosealba, gave Adán an abrazo, rubbed the boys' crewcuts with his large hands and then grabbed a fistful of apricots.

"Well, hate to eat and run. But my brother wants me to help him fix his car." Joe turned to Beatriz and kissed her. "I'll be back around four. Hope you're all done by then. You know I'm dangerous in a kitchen. You don't want me . . . 'helping.'"

"Yeah. You're like a bull in a china shop. But we can always count on you to eat everything in sight," Beatriz said.

With a wave, Joe left. Bea took a kerchief out of her back pocket and tied it around her thick, curly dark hair.

"She looks exactly like you," Luli said to Rosealba.

Beatriz beamed. "Everyone tells us that. Now if I could only cook like my mom. Joe says the City of Albuquerque should use my tortillas for manhole covers."

"Awww, m'ija, you're still learning."

"Yeah. Maybe in another sixty years I'll get the hang of it."

The jam making went on all day. Under Rosealba's watchful eye, the cooks took turns stirring boiling cauldrons of fruit, sugar, and pectin outside on the grill. "Make sure that stuff don't stick to the bottom of the pot," she warned, continually checking up on her staff. "It can burn real fast."

As the jam thickened, Luli watched Rosealba toss a few apricot pits into the bubbling pot, adding a couple of sticks of cinnamon and a few cloves. "What's all that for?"

"Flavor. Apricot pits smell like almonds. Here, crack one open. Some cooks take out the white nut inside and put a few in with the jam. They add a little almond taste, but they also contain some kind of poison."

"Cyanide?" Adán offered. "Let's skip that part. Don't want to kill everybody."

"I like to put a little almond liquor into a few of the jars. But we mark those. We don't want Flip getting no jam with the booze in it," Rosealba cautioned.

"What about the lemons?" Luli asked.

"Could you squeeze them and pick out the seeds? Last thing before we pour the jam into the jars and put the lids on, I add the lemon juice. Apricots have citric acid, but just in case, it don't hurt to add more. It helps keep the jam from browning on top."

Rosealba processed quart jars seven at a time in a boiling water bath. After fifteen minutes, she removed them and set them down carefully on wire racks. Meanwhile, Beatriz and Luli filled more sterile glass containers, both quart and pint-sized. They wiped dripped jam off the rim, dipping the cloth in boiling water to clean it. Next, they put on the lids and loosely screwed the bands to hold them on.

Around one-thirty, Beatriz said, "Mom, I'm hungry. Can't we take a break? I'd kill for a bean burrito."

"Paciencia, hija. We only have about two more loads to go."

Beatriz groaned and went back to carefully ladling jam.

Finally Rosealba gently lowered the last rack into the boiling water and set the timer.

"Hooray!" Beatriz yelled. "Where's my lunch? I think I'm gonna faint."

"All right. Now I'll make burritos. But while I'm cooking, could you scoop the leftover jam in some of those plastic containers? When they're cool, put tops on them, and take them to the outside fridge. I think we have enough canned to last us through to summer."

"Of what year?" Beatriz laughed.

Luli counted the neat orange jars sitting on wire racks around the kitchen. "Wow, Rosealba, you've got twenty-one quarts and forty-two pints. What a haul."

"I told you, Luli, we don't always have a apricot crop, so when we do, we have to make the best of it."

Joe roared up the hill on his Harley and walked into the kitchen just as Rosealba was putting a plate of burritos in the center of the table. "Excellent timing, huh?" he said, reaching for one.

Beatriz gently slapped his hand. "Hey—we haven't had our lunch yet."

"There's plenty for everyone," Rosealba said. "I'll make more if we run out."

After two bean burritos, Luli was ready for a shower and a nap. "What hard work," she said, placing her borrowed apron in the washing machine with the jam-sticky wiping cloths and potholders.

"Yes, but this is so much better than anything you can buy at the store," Rosealba said. "We don't put in as much sugar as the commercial kitchens. They use about equal measures of sugar and fruit. So sweet it make your teeth ache."

"Yeah," Bea said. "And they charge a lot for it. When I was in Kaune's last week, I looked at apricot jam from

France. It was more than six dollars for a teensy jar. Not even a pint."

"Bea, give Luli one of those plastic containers with the fresh jam. It will last for weeks in the refrigerator. You come by tomorrow, Luli, and I'll give you some canned ones to take back to your place. We can't move the jars until they pop. That tells us they've sealed. Sometimes they pop right away, and sometimes they don't pop until morning."

"And sometimes they don't pop at all. Which means you have to put the jam in the fridge and eat it up soon," Beatriz said.

"Tough job, but somebody's gotta do it," Joe said, volunteering.

Luli accepted a dozen pints from Rosealba. She labeled them and lined them up on a shelf in the pantry, front row and center where she could admire them. She sent jars to each of her kids and her mother. Allie called her from Camp Manitowish. "Wow, Mom. You made this?"

"Not by myself. It was all the Alires and me. The fruit's from their apricot tree."

"It's fabulous! My friend Aynur came to my cabin for tea, and we had some on toast. She's from Turkey, and she said it was the best apricot jam she's ever had."

"Really?"

"Yup. In fact, she taught me a Turkish proverb: 'Bundan iyisi Şam'da kayısı.'"

"I'm afraid to ask what that means."

"She says literally it means the only thing better than this is an apricot in Damascus. Basically, it's like when we're totally thrilled or pleased with something and we say: 'It doesn't get any better than this.'"

"I love that. Tell it to me again, slowly. I'm going to write it down and memorize it."

"She also wants to know if the jam has any secret ingredients."

"Sweat, dear. Lots of it. That's the special flavoring."

17

· · · · · · ·

Luli enjoyed her job at Beto's shop. Not many people stopped by and those who did mostly headed for the studio. A few tourists wandered in off the street. They'd pick things up, put them down in the wrong place, or ask mostly silly questions. More than once, people wanted to know if she had made all the obviously antique furniture herself. She rarely sold anything—maybe every day or two, usually a small item—a decorated earthenware platter from Mexico, a Oaxaca basket, or a little silver cup. If a customer wanted information, she summoned Beto and listened to what he told them.

Part of her job was to sign for UPS, FedEx and DHL packages from New York, L.A., Dallas, or from out of the country: Mexico City, Madrid, Buenos Aires, London. Beto unpacked them in his studio. Sometimes the shipping companies picked up boxes Beto usually packed himself. "Is an art, the packing. Sometime I show you."

A friend of his came in carrying a breadbox sized wooden container with narrow drawers, one of them without its front. Luli guessed it was a jewelry box. Beto was pleased when he saw it. He slapped his friend on the back and gave him two one hundred dollar bills. Luli was surprised. The box was plain, covered with chipped white paint, and missing a couple of drawer pulls and one of its ball feet. Two hundred dollars seemed like a lot for a box that was basically a wreck.

Later, Luli went into the workshop to ask Beto a question about a nineteenth century Mexican armoire a customer was interested in. Sitting on top of his worktable was the box. Beto had stripped off the white paint and was fitting a sanded piece of old wood to the drawer that was missing a panel.

"What do you call those corners, Beto? You told me once, but I forgot."

"Is the dovetailing, the ensambladura in Spanish. Traditional technique for when people don't have the nails. This cofre, this box, is late 1700s Bolivia."

"Really? It's that old? It's plain, but pretty in a way."

"When I finish, is much, much more beautiful," he said with a grin.

At the end of Luli's second week, Beto wrote her a check for the sixty hours she worked—$660. She was thrilled. She walked downtown and opened an account at the First National Bank. Then she bought herself an ice cream at the Plaza Bakery and raspberry bars for Adán, Rosealba, and Flip.

As she was leaving for work Monday morning, the bank called. "We're sorry, Mrs. Russell, but the check you deposited from Mr. Colilla didn't clear. Your balance is $22.35."

Luli was almost too worried to be angry. She walked to the store and found Beto in his back room studio. She tapped on the open door. All the hombres looked up from their various projects.

"Can I see you for a second?"

Beto put down his cigarette and followed her into the gallery.

"I hate to have to tell you, but the check you wrote me Friday bounced," she said solemnly.

He shrugged. "Just say no to worry, Luli."

"But, now I don't have any money in the bank, and I have bills to pay. In fact, I've already written a couple of checks on this account."

"Luli, Luli, Luli. What is a check? Is a promise to pay. I promise to pay you!"

"Beto, I can't pay my bills with promises."

He grinned nonchalantly and walked into the studio. She heard a flurry of Spanish, some raucous laughter, and soon Beto returned with a stack of bills. Wordlessly, he counted out $660, handed it to her, patted her cheek, and went back to his workbench.

When she told the Alires about Beto's bounced check. Adán nodded. "Yeah, that's his reputation around town. His checks are usually made of rubber. I meant to tell you. A friend of mine, Lalo, worked on Beto's car. Nice old

Mustang. Beto paid him with one of those 'promises to pay,' and Lalo couldn't squeeze any real money out of him. Finally, he went to Beto's house in the middle of the night, pushed the car downhill, hotwired it, and drove off. Beto didn't get his car back until he paid Lalo with cash.

"But otherwise, people say he's a true artist with a great deal of talent, a nice guy. He's had the same girlfriend for many years, and he and his Chilean friends stay out of trouble. Alls you have to do is ask for your pay in real money."

Sometimes, one of the back room crew took a battered acoustic guitar down from the wall and began to play. Others joined in, singing plaintive songs filled with longing. One would beat on the dinged up aluminum pot Beto used to boil water for making mate. The others clapped a complex syncopated rhythm.

"Your music is very beautiful," Luli told them. "But it's so sad."

"We are all exiles from our country, señora. We are miss our families, our sweethearts, our homes. The music help us remember. Or maybe it help us forget," said Paco.

Ché said, "I was a labor leader in Buenos Aires. The dictator kill my colegas, so I leave to Chile. Bad idea. Then a dictator take over that country and I have to leave Chile también."

The men laughed bitterly.

Ché pointed to Kiko. "His father, he was in the estadio in Santiago in 1973 when the militares smash the hands of

Victor Jara, our most best músico, then they kill him. They kill Kiko's father, also a famous musician."

Like most North Americans, Luli knew next to nothing about Latin American politics. "But, why did you and your friends have to leave your country?"

"The U.S. give money to the militares to throw over our government, which is the democratically elect government of Salvador Allende, but they think he is communist. They shoot him, the presidente, in his office, then they say he kill himself."

"What? The U.S.? But that's terrible!"

"Si, señora. They put many people in prison. They torture them. They drop peoples out of helicópteros into the ocean. The fascitas say my friends they are communistas. But they are artists, intellectuals. No matter, they must leave Chile or the militares kill them. Kiko, he is a wonderful músico of the flamenco style, like his papá, a gitano—how you say?—a yipsy. But the fascistas hate the yipsies. He have to leave too. I am live here, so they come to Santa Fe. We help each other."

When business was slow and the store was clean, Luli read Beto's books about Spanish Colonial art and Latin American culture. She'd never studied either, but since it had become important for her job, she devoured his reference works. She also began to pick up more Spanish.

Beto listened to her telling a customer about a beautiful trestle table, nodding as she explained the term marquetería, pointed out the various types of wood used in the inlay, and described the piece as late colonial Mexican, probably from Michoacán.

When he left, promising to return soon with his wife, Beto congratulated Luli. "You have learn so much, very fast. You impress me."

She smiled. "Muchas gracias, Beto."

18

· · · · · · ·

FRIDAY AFTERNOON, LULI SLOWLY CLIMBED THE HILL
carrying a bag of groceries. It had been a busy day at the
shop, cleaning and moving furniture around with Beto
and a couple of the chilenos. She was tired and filthy and
longing for a shower. With each step the sack grew heavier.
At the top of the hill, she noticed dozens of cars and a few
motorcycles parked around the Alire's house. "Must be a
party," she thought. A huge red pickup zoomed into the
driveway and skidded to a halt. A young woman, her face
flushed, her eyes streaming mascara, got out and raced into
the yard. It was Rosita, Adán and Rosealba's older daughter.

"Rosita?" Luli called. "Is something wrong?"

"It's my sister Bea. And Joe. Some fucking asshole
T-boned them and they're dead!" She clapped her hand
over her mouth and ran into the house sobbing.

Luli dropped her sack; cans rolled out of the split bag.
"Oh, my God." She closed her eyes; she could barely breathe.
"Those wonderful kids? Just weeks before their wedding?"

She stood dumb, immobile as a stone pillar in the driveway of the Alire's house, remembering lovely, vivacious

Bea and her adoring fiancé. So suddenly gone? Adán and Rosealba had now lost two children and Joe, who was like a son to them. How would they ever survive this enormous loss?

She debated whether to follow Rosita, but this was obviously an intimate time for the family, not one she felt she should intrude on. The wailing she heard from the house tore at her heart. She ached for the Alires and Joe's family. As she walked toward her door, Basura appeared at her side and listlessly wagged his tail. Luli lifted his jaw, peered into his sorrowful eyes, and stroked his head. "Oh, Basura, this is so awful." The dog blinked as if he understood, wandered back home, and flopped down in the grass beside the porch.

After Luli methodically put her food away, she sat on the sofa, too shocked to move, as dusk deepened into night. She could hear cars and trucks arriving and leaving the Alires', a few motorcycles rumbling. She heard a timid knock.

"Who is it?" She called out, getting up from the sofa and turning on lights.

"It's me, Daniel," a young voice said.

Luli opened the door. The boy looked so small, so sad, she knelt down and folded him in her arms.

"Gramita asked me to tell you that . . ."

"I know about your Aunt Bea and Joe," she said, tears sliding down her cheeks. "Please tell you family my heart goes out to them, to all of you. What a horrible thing!"

Daniel nodded solemnly. "Uncle Joe was gonna take me for a ride on his new motorcycle this weekend." He sniffled, then remembered his errand, and swept his hand across his wet cheeks and runny nose. "Gramita says to tell you the mass is on Tuesday at the Cathedral, at ten o'clock."

"I'll be there. Thank you. You're all in my thoughts. I hope they'll let me know if I can be helpful in any way."

Luli couldn't think of food for herself but she did the Midwestern neighborly thing and baked a triple recipe of scalloped potatoes with ingredients she had on hand. When she'd made the dish before, the Alires enjoyed it. She carried the casserole to the house and knocked on the open door. A teary-eyed young man in biker leathers opened the screen, a bit unsteady on his feet.

"Please give this to Rosealba," she said, setting the casserole on a bench by the doorway and slipping off her oven mitts. "Here, use these. The dish is very hot."

He nodded, slipped the gloves on his huge hands, and carried the food.inside.

Luli sat in a pew at the back of the crowded church. Two matching bronze caskets adorned with bouquets of vanilla white and fuchsia roses filled the center aisle at the nave. The priest, a red-haired Anglo, stood with his hand resting on one of the caskets and spoke of the couple in a mixture of English and hesitant, heavily accented Spanish. Although he was saying kind words about the couple, Luli could tell he had never met them.

"The loss of these two young lives, though it fills us with sorrow, is a clear indication of the will of God, who does not ask of us sacrifices greater than we can bear," he told the congregation. "We must all recognize the hand of God that may, at any moment, reach into our lives and snatch away what we hold most dear. Despite our pain, we must accept His will. For the love of God overshadows everything else."

"Horseshit!" Luli thought. "God's will, huh? I've had enough of that to last me lifetimes—and the Alires, even more so."

After the priest finished, he retired to the altar, and began the funeral mass in a practiced drone while mariachis in the choir loft played soft melodies on guitars and violins. Even when people went to the railing for communion and returned to their pews, Luli didn't see anyone she knew except the Alire family. She watched pallbearers solemnly carry the caskets past her to hearses waiting at the curb, flanked by an honor guard of bikers. Over the grumble of motorcycle engines, the musicians standing outside played "Sombras," Bea's favorite Javier Solís song. A stream of weeping mourners filed past. Among the last to leave the church were Rosealba and Adán, flanked by Rosita and Arturo. Her eyes red-rimmed and puffy, Rosealba held her husband's hand. He looked gray and drawn. Flip shuffled along behind them, his head bent, a worn suit hanging loosely from his thin shoulders. Rosealba stopped when she saw Luli and the women embraced.

"I have no words to tell you how sad I am for you and your entire family." Luli sobbed. "I would have come immediately, but I didn't feel right invading your privacy at such a time. I hope you understand."

Rosealba nodded. "Of course I do." She gave Luli's hand a squeeze. "Please come have coffee with me soon. And thank you for the delicious papas. They were gone very quick."

Luli waited a few days, then stopped by the Alires' after work with a bag of Mexican wedding cookies she knew Rosealba liked. As they shared a pot of coffee, the two of them sat on the sofa under the wall of family photographs. A gilt-edged mass card was inserted into a corner of the frame and a few roses drooped over the glass of the photo of Bea and Joe on their Harley.

"The man who kill Beatriz and Joe is a retired pastor," Rosealba said wearily. "He's eighty-eight and he was driving a new Lincoln. Rosie and Joe were going up Central Avenue in Albuquerque near the university on Joe's bike, helmets on and everything. He was taking her to chemistry lab. That preacher drove right through a stop sign. It happen when classes were changing, so lots of people saw the accident. Now his church's lawyers are trying to sue us." Rosealba was shaking with fury.

"They're going to sue *you*?" Luli jumped up from the sofa. "That's garbage! I'd think it would be the other way around—you and Joe's parents sue the pastor—big time. He killed your kids."

"The cops don't even give him a ticket. He say he black out because he's diabetic and that's why he go through the stop sign. Well, if that minister's so sick, why is he driving? Maybe he hit the accelerator instead of the brake? A student who saw the crash said the driver's eyes were wide open and his mouth, and he looked real surprised. I guess he's some big deal in his church, and he's the mayor's uncle, and maybe the cops feel sorry for him. The lawyers say the accident was Joe's fault, for speeding and driving reckless. They're lying. He was always careful, especially with my girl on the bike with him." Rosealba's eyes watered.

"There are witnesses?"

"Yes. The student got a list of people who saw the accident, with their names, emails, and phone numbers. The first person to try to help was a nurse in Bea's class. He's upset bad. But he called and told us Bea and Joe died right away." Rivers of tears coursed down Rosealba's cheeks. "I thank God for that. Now they're in heaven together. At least they're not vegetables in no nursing home."

"Have you got a lawyer?"

"We sure do—Sammy Pacheco. His sister, Inés, is the doctor taking care of Flip. Sammy's awful smart. He went to the Harvard law school. Flip says it's the best one. Sammy told us that preacher's lawyers think we're a bunch of dumb spicks and they can scare us into paying for damage to the old man's car. Joe's insurance don't want to pay nothing either. We don't care about the money. It won't bring our kids back to us. But we care about what's right and what's wrong."

"The truly wrong thing is he shouldn't have been driving, and two wonderful young people are dead because of him. Has he apologized to any of you?"

"Not one peep out of him. Some Christian he is. Bea's friend at the accident, the nursing student, say the driver wasn't hurt at all. He have an airbag in his car. But he talk on and on about his new car being all smashed up, and how his glasses got broke."

Luli shook her head. "I can't believe that's what he cares about—a car, his glasses. He must be totally senile. How could anybody even think about replaceable things after killing two innocent people?"

"I don't get it neither," Rosealba said.

"What does Sammy tell you about the lawyers?"

"He says we don't need to do nothing. He's handling all of it—Joe's insurance company, the pastor's insurance company, the church's lawyers. The day after the accident one of the insurance people call here, and she was real nasty to me."

"Incredible. They have no right to contact you. You don't deserve any crap from anybody."

"That's exactly what Sammy told us. He says if one of them calls again, we tell them his phone number and hang up."

"Please let me know if there's anything I can do. I am so, so sorry." Luli wrapped her arms around a sobbing Rosealba.

Allie came to visit her mother after she finished her camp counselor's job, before she moved to Chicago with Craig. Luli was thrilled to see her. She missed her kids terribly.

"Don't worry, Mom, you're suffering from Empty Nest Syndrome. It's quite common among women in your situation, but rarely fatal."

"Thank you so much, Doctor Russell. You and your sibs can help cure me by coming to visit really often."

"It's a deal. I totally love your adobe and I haven't even begun to explore this town. Craig's going to love it."

"Maybe you two should visit at Christmas. I hear it's remarkably festive."

"That's a possibility. And your painting. Wow! I can see you're really getting somewhere. No more cows and barns and grim weather, huh?"

Late that night Luli thought she heard screaming. She sat up in bed. No, she wasn't having a nightmare. Someone was yelling, and it sounded like Rosealba. She hastily threw on a bathrobe over her pajamas and ran outside in her slippers. A battered black lowrider was disappearing around the bend of Alire Circle and Rosealba was shaking her fist at it, yelling something in Spanish that included expletives Luli had learned from being around the chilenos.

"Rosealba! What's going on?"

"La Muerte. She has already steal my kids, she can't have Adán too."

"Let's go inside," she said, putting her arm around Rosealba's shoulders.

Allie came out of Luli's house, wearing a long T-shirt, hugging herself against the night's chill. "What's happening?" she asked in a sleepy voice.

"Go back to bed, honey. I'll handle this. Don't worry."

Inside the Alire's house, Luli put water on for tea. Rosealba sat at the kitchen table, shaking and muttering to herself in a babble of Spanish and English. Luli took off her bathrobe and draped it gently around Rosealba.

"Do you want to tell me what's wrong? Should I call Rosita? Or Dr. Pacheco?"

"No, no," Rosealba said. Looking down at her clenched fists, she spoke slowly. "I'm taking care of Danny. He have a high fever, from the malaria he catch in the war. It comes back to him a lot, gives him the shakes, terrible headaches. When he get this way, I put the cold cloths on him when he's hot, and blankets when he's cold. So tonight I'm sitting with him and I hear a car outside. I go look out the bedroom window. Somebody in one of them jackets that goes over your head . . ."

"A sweatshirt? A hoodie?"

"Yeah, I guess that's what you call them. The person come out of this beat up old car carrying a long stick with a curved knife on the end, like we use to cut the hay..."

"A scythe?"

"She start walking to our front door. I don't see no face. I run to the window and I look out again. Now I see a skeleton face inside the hoodie, and when she knock, I open the door. She start to come in and I slam the door hard into that face. Real hard. I hope I break some bones! It was La Muerte."

Luli knew the word. "Death? You saw a figure of death?"

"Yes. She come to take my Danny. I scream for her to go away. 'You have my niños, my parents, you can't have my husband.' I guess it work. She go get in that carrucha and drive away."

"I saw the car leave, but I couldn't see who was driving."

"Te digo—it was La Muerte."

"Are you sure I shouldn't call Inés?"

"No, I am OK. Danny's not so bad. I seen him worse. If he's still with a high fever in the morning, then I call her.

"You go home, Luli. I'm settle down. I'm calm. This manzanilla tea helps. Thank you for coming. Maybe you help scare off the puta cabrona. Oops, I don't usually use them words, but you know what I mean."

"I certainly do. Promise me you'll call if you need me. Any time. For anything, even just to talk."

"What was that all about?" Allie asked when her mother came home.

Luli related Rosealba's story, adding "I saw the car."

"Do you really believe Death was visiting the Alires?"

Luli shrugged. "You know, the older I become, the more open I am to things I don't totally understand."

"There seems to be a lot of weirdness here in New Mexico."

"Yes. Well, weird for us Midwesterners, anyway. Maybe that's why I like it here."

19

· · · · · · ·

Luli was walking home to Alire Circle after work when a shiny new blue Chevrolet sedan slowed down as it passed her. She glanced at the driver. Although he sped up and turned right at the next intersection, she was fairly sure it was a man she'd seen standing outside the shop a time or two, always wearing a bill cap and a pinstriped shirt. A few days later, she was crossing the plaza to deposit her pay at the bank when she thought she saw him again, eating at Roque's carnitas wagon, salsa dripping down his shirt, adding to its stripes. As soon as he saw her looking at him, he turned away.

Beto trusted Luli with a key to the front door, although not the one to the studio. She didn't mind; it was his sanctuary. When she opened the gallery one morning in July, Mr. Stripey, as she had come to call him, was leaning against a tree across the street, watching. With a portraitist's eye she paid close attention to his features: an angular jaw, a graying dash of a moustache above the tight, thin seam of his mouth, high cheekbones framing small eyes that gleamed like black glass, a prominent Adam's apple jutting from his long chicken neck, a tuft of gray chest hair sprouting from the top of his green striped shirt. As she studied him, he jerked his cap down over his thick eyebrows, put on a pair of aviator sunglasses and briskly walked away.

What is with this guy? Luli wondered. Is he casing the place? Stalking me? She told Beto about him.

He thought about it, took a drag on his cigarette, and shrugged. "This town full of locos," he said.

But Luli felt he was more bothered than she was.

Rosealba knocked at Luli's house as dusk was falling, the August sky a vivid orange and lavender behind silhouetted trees. "Come on in," Luli said, opening the door for her. "Wow," she said noting Rosealba's big smile. "What's up? I haven't seen you grinning like that in way too long. Have a seat."

"We're done!" Rosealba said joyfully, waving her hands in the air, dancing on her toes. "The whole lawsuit got resolved today, and we don't have to have no trial. A friend of our family who's a very well respected retired judge in Albuquerque, Judge Álvaro Benavides, help Sammy out with the case. Maybe that's why it got resolve so fast. He said the ministers' lawyers were real ugly, the worst bunch he's ever been up against. Judge Benavides told him he should make a complaint about them to the bar—I guess that's the lawyers' union."

"Did they pull the pastor's driver's license?"

"Yes, they did. It was the first thing we want Sammy to try for, and it was part of the settlement. He's not going to kill nobody else with his big car.

"Anyways, it's over. ¡Ya basta! The insurance companies have to pay a lot of money to us and Joe's family. I mean, a lot. I almost fell over when Sammy told us how much. But we don't want no money. Joe's family says the same thing. It's not going to bring back our kids. We're setting up a scholarship fund in Bea's name at the university for nursing students, and one in Joe's memory at the community college, for kids who want to be mechanics. Our whole family's thrilled. We pay for the funeral and we pay Sammy, and maybe now we can sleep better."

Rosealba hesitated, then looked down and wept. "But I'll never see my Beatriz and Joe again!"

"Not in this life, anyway."

"I guess we have to believe they are always with us."

PART III

20

. . . .

IN MID-AUGUST, BETO AND HIS FRIENDS WORKED long hours repairing and cleaning paintings, santos, masks, furniture. "We go to the Antique Ethnographic Show downtown next weekend," he explained to Luli. "More than 150 dealers sell antique stuff from the many countries, the tribes peoples. You can come help me with the sales? I pay you extra. Is very interesting. You like it. Marvelous art you never see other places, not even in museums."

The morning before the show opened in Sweeney Center, Beto stormed into the shop waving a newspaper in the air, his face red. Luli didn't understand exactly what he was saying to his friends, but she could tell he was furious and using a lot of bad words.

Later, he apologized. "Sorry I not say hello when I come in, linda. I am so mad with the stupid stuff this jackass say. Here, you read it."

He paced up and down the gallery while she read the article in *Pasatiempo*, the paper's Friday arts magazine. The writer said that the antique ethnographic art business worldwide was under fire from diplomats, academics, and archaeologists. Officials from Immigration and Customs

Enforcement stated that much of the antique art offered for sale in Santa Fe galleries or shows like the Antique Ethnographic Show was stolen from churches, museums, or archaeological sites.

In a sidebar, the paper published an ominous sounding "Red List" of forbidden items: k'eros, Mayan jade pendants, Mezcal figures.

Luli recognized very few of the things on the list. "What's a k'ero?"

"A wood cup from the Incas, for drinking the chicha beer. No big deal. They still make them, out of one piece of wood. Maybe thirty people in the U.S. knows what is a k'ero. This article is a pendejada! The federales want try to make us the same thieves like the peoples who dig up the Indian graves in Utah. Why they don't go after Sotheby's or Christie's for the artefactos they sell for many, many thousands to rich people, to museums? Or chase real criminals—the ones who sell guns and explosives to Mexico, smuggle inmigrantes or ship the drogas into the U.S. and pay off federales with mordidas? No, they try to make people not go to the show, not buy our stuff.

"Some of this is so bad writing, it make me to laugh. Your government forbid us to sell the San Agustín statues from Colombia. ¡Genial! Those are very big rocks, some are bigger than houses, weigh many, many tons. People not to buy paintings from Mexico or Guatemala or religious esculptures because they are stolen? Is wrong. Is bullshit. The families sell the old things, like from the grandmother in the U.S. when she die. Or the paintings are made yesterday. Who know the difference?

"Is paternalismo. Your government think it help save stupid poor countries' patrimonio, then the countries let the U.S. put soldiers there, and the drug airplanes, and the DEA. They save everybody from themself. The professors in the university, they think they know my business? They don't know nothing. ¡Mierda, pura mierda!"

Beto and his pals spent Friday carefully transporting select merchandise from the store to the booth in Sweeney Center and setting it up like a small shop with Luli's help. Other vendors were doing the same. Soon the former high school gym was transformed into a bustling bazaar of exotic goods. Luli placed a huge bouquet of deep red roses from her garden in a Talavera pitcher on a carved table draped with an antique Chilean poncho, and filled a colonial Bolivian silver dish with Hershey's Kisses. Everything gleamed in the spotlights—silver candlesticks, cups, and platters, polychrome santos, furniture, Talavera pottery. Beto put out additional merchandise, costly one of a kind items she'd never seen for sale in the gallery.

Shopkeepers busied themselves setting up their booths before the Friday night gala, stopping occasionally to discuss the newspaper article. One, who had been a cultural attaché in various Latin American countries, told Beto, "This is what we used to call a puff piece, something a government official wrote and sent to the newspapers as a press release. I'll bet this came directly from ICE's PR office. Timed to coincide with the opening of this show—perfect. Scare off all the customers, will ya? That writer copied and pasted the whole thing into his column and put his name on it. If he'd done his homework and interviewed a few of us who truly know this business, the article wouldn't have appeared. It's the laziest form of journalism."

Opening night, a charity benefit at $200 a head, was like no party Luli had ever attended. Hundreds of stylishly dressed patrons strolled through booths, champagne was flowing, and hors d'oeuvres fast disappearing from trays passed around by waiters in black tie. Revelers paraded up and down the aisles, stopping to greet friends effusively, or gush about something for sale. Luli wore her best dress, a form-fitting red shantung sheath. Beto loaned her elegant fifties Taxco silver jewelry and swathed her shoulders in a beautifully embroidered black and red manta from Bolivia that matched her dress perfectly.

"Ooooh, you are fabulosa, Luli," Beto said, stepping back to admire her. "¡Deliciosa! You stop the traffic for sure."

Luli knew she looked terrific, but she was clearly underdressed by Santa Fe standards. Both men and women sported pounds of silver and turquoise Indian jewelry, feathers, beads, handmade shirts, dazzling shawls, vintage clothing, turbans, rhinestone cowboy boots—even jingling spurs. Luli thought many of the men were flashier than the women. She'd certainly never seen anything like it in Green Bay.

Sales were brisk. Beto, dressed in an embroidered guayabera shirt and smelling of lemon cologne, was at his most gregarious. He kissed all the women on the cheek, embraced the men in hearty abrazos, and chatted up potential customers as he rarely did in the shop.

Visitors to the booth were particularly attracted to a small 18th century traveling desk, a bargueño, with gaily painted and gilded dancing figures in colonial dress cavorting across its dropleaf front. Luli watched as Beto lifted the lid by its ironwork hasp to show a customer its interior. Inside were a number of tiny drawers, their facades painted and gilded with floral flourishes and scrolls, more dancers, birds, llamas, deer, and other native fauna.

A distinguished looking elderly man in a tuxedo with a nineteenth century Saltillo sarape over one shoulder, took Beto aside for a chat while Luli waited on other customers, gave out business cards and chocolates, and invited people to visit the shop. The two men conferred for some time. After the customer left, Beto took a red SOLD tag out of his pocket and laid it on top of the bargueño, his eyes shining and wide as his smile.

"$15,000!" he whispered to Luli. "And it go to a museum."

Luli spent all of Saturday and Sunday at the show. When she could slip away from the booth, leaving Beto or one of the chilenos in charge, she wandered the aisles in wonder. Vendors offered beautiful antique textiles, exotic masks, tribal jewelry, paintings, and any number of objects she couldn't begin to identify from all around the world. The salespeople were happy to provide her with information and let her handle even fragile, very expensive objects. Luli was thrilled. "This is like an intensive weekend seminar in the art of the world," she told Beto.

"Is the best, Luli. I promise you don't see nothing like this no place."

The Saturday visitors were unlike Friday night's gala crowd, slower moving, not dressed with as much splash. Some were obviously window-shopping; others were more serious and deliberate. Luli noticed a man in a light blue short-sleeved shirt and navy slacks carefully inspecting every inch of Beto's eight by ten foot booth. He even stooped to look under the poncho covering the table, all the while declining to make eye contact or respond to Luli's offers to provide information.

"Sir, you seem to be looking for something specific," she said with exasperation. "If you tell me what it is, maybe I can help you find it."

The man mumbled something.

"Excuse me? I didn't hear you."

"A chacmool," he said more clearly, looking at her as if she were dumber than a box of rocks.

Luli was embarrassed. "I'm afraid I don't know what that is. The owner is right across the aisle. I'll ask him. Please tell me again what you're looking for."

"A chacmool!" he said loudly.

Vendors within earshot turned to stare, then broke into grins. A half-dozen of them converged on Beto's booth.

"So you're looking for a chacmool?" the former diplomat asked the man, nudging a colleague in the ribs. More dealers came up. "He's looking for a chacmool," they told one another and laughed.

Luli had no idea why the dealers were making fun of the man. By now his face was flushed and he was scowling. Noticing the hubbub, Beto returned. His colleagues gathered closer. "This is gonna be good," one said in eager anticipation.

Beto walked up to the man and stood inches from his face. Surprised by his aggressiveness, the man backed up. He looked a little uneasy, but was doing his best to stay in control.

"You make a joke?" Beto asked loudly, his voice tinged with anger. "You know what is a chacmool?"

Activity in the nearby booths stopped as people in all directions focused on Beto and the customer. The merchants were clearly enjoying the spectacle.

The man stood his ground. "I sure do, compadre," he retorted smugly. "It's one of those Inca god gizmos, pre-Columbian."

Beto shook his head in disgust and narrowed his eyes. "You a cop?" he asked in a booming voice.

The man was taken aback but quickly recovered his composure. "No, I'm not a cop," he said sarcastically.

The two men glared at each other, facing off like warring tomcats.

"Actually," the man added, "I'm a federal prosecutor. With an art degree from Pratt."

Beto moved even closer to him. "Lárgate, you fucking idiot!" he hissed. "You need go back to school, chota. Maybe one where I am the teacher."

The man's jaw dropped, he turned as red as Luli's roses, and stalked off. The vendors whistled and hooted, applauding as he rapidly elbowed his way through the crowds and disappeared.

Luli was flabbergasted, as were many of the customers within hearing distance. Beto shook his head, muttering to himself in Spanish. He turned toward the aisle, and spoke loud enough for everyone to hear.

"Ladies and gentlemens! The chacmool this *federal* look for in my booth is a immense Toltec or post-classic Mayan god figure, a god for the rain. Is from Mexico, not Peru, like this pendejo think. Is a stone figure of many tons, maybe six feet, eight feet long. He lie down, his back lift up and his knees, he have big ears, his face turn to you, he staring. His hands hold a plate on his stomach. For the sacrifice. Maybe have a heart in it once. Maybe you see this esculpture in a Kahlúa ad?

"That cabrón think I have hide a chacmool in my booth? Is easier to have a elephant in here. The Queen Mary ship. The Brooklyn Bridge. Hah! Maybe he want to buy that! I am happy to sell it to him."

The former diplomat clapped Beto on the back. "Good job, hombre. I had to work with those customs jerks sometimes. They sure know how to throw their weight around, but they don't know jack shit about art."

The entertainment at an end, the spectators went back to business.

The Monday after the show, a constant stream of people flowed through the gallery, wanting to talk to Beto. Traders tried to sell him items they hadn't sold during the weekend. Other visitors were out-of-towners who had seen Beto's booth in Sweeney Center and wanted to visit his shop. Luli didn't have time for lunch. Sales were almost as brisk as they had been at the show.

"What a busy time," Beto said. "Take a couple of days off, linda. Maybe I don't work either. We put a sign on the door. I see you Thursday, no?"

Luli didn't need to be told she was tired. The weekend had been exciting, but exhausting—packing and unpacking, setting up the booth, waiting on people for two full days. Then after the show, the repacking and unpacking back at the gallery, putting displays together again. She'd been on her feet for four days straight.

Tuesday, she slept in and decided to go for a hike, taking advantage of the sunny, mild, mid-August morning to visit Bandelier National Monument. She made a picnic lunch, tucked her sketchpad and watercolors into a tote, and pointed Mrs. Phlegmish toward the Jémez mountains, northwest of Santa Fe. For several hours, Luli ambled along paths through a hidden complex of archaeological ruins deep in Frijoles Canyon, where early Pueblo people had lived between 1100 and 1300 AD, only to mysteriously abandon the place. Both sides of the narrow leafy valley sloped to a creek in its center. Beneath box elders, ponderosa pines, and Gambel's oaks, clear water tumbled over stones and glinted in the sunlight. Luli followed other hikers along the pathways leading to cliff dwellings in the north wall of the canyon. She watched as parents urged their eager kids up peeled pole ladders to little caves native people had long ago dug in the tufa of the cliff face and used as shelters, sleeping quarters, and storage rooms. Once the youngsters were up the ladders, the adults down below invariably directed them to look out of the tiny doorways into their cameras.

While she watched the families enjoy themselves, Luli grew nostalgic for her own kids. Although they were all now young adults, they would have enjoyed this place as much as any five-year-olds.

Along the trail, she stopped from time to time to sit on a rock or stump and dash off a quick impressionistic study of circular kivas, cliff dwellings, the pock-marked tufa, the scraggly pines above pitched at impossible angles on the cliff sides, patches of the sky, and its ever changing display of clouds moving in. Passersby peered over her shoulder.

"You're pretty good, ma'am," a man in a cowboy hat said. "Are you an artist?"

"Not a real one," Luli said.

"Well, I'm no critic, but seems to me like you've captured the feel of this place."

"Yeah," his little girl said. "You're a good drawer."

"Is your painting for sale?" asked the cowboy.

"Uh . . . I hadn't thought about it, but . . . sure. Why not?"

"How about $200 for it? Plus your autograph, of course."

"You're serious?"

"Yup, I am." He counted out four fifties and handed them to her.

Luli signed the watercolor and gave it to him. "Don't roll it up yet. It's not quite dry."

"Gotcha. Thanks a bunch."

"Thank you." Luli replied. "This is my first sale in New Mexico. Whoopee!"

She sat at a picnic table along the stream eating her sandwich and carrot sticks under the watchful eye of an Abert's squirrel. As she tossed him tidbits, she continued to glow, still amazed. Could she actually make it as an artist in her new home?

Driving back to town, she reflected on her day at Bandelier. No history class she had ever taken mentioned the pre-conquest civilizations of the American Southwest, their art, their architecture, or the skills they had developed to survive in a difficult climate. The peaceful valley, the sacred kivas, the beautiful pottery and baskets in the Park's small museum, and the mysterious pictographs the Anasazi painted on the cliffs and stucco walls of their rooms intrigued her. She resolved to learn more about the "old ones" and the other places they left behind long before the Spanish came. She also wanted to come back again to paint.

The next afternoon, Luli strolled downtown to the library to look for information on Bandelier Monument and the people who had lived there. The library staff suggested a number of books, including *The Delight Makers*, an historical novel written by Adolf Bandelier, the Swiss archaeologist who, in the 1880s, brought attention to the ruins that now bear his name. She spent the rest of the afternoon in the back yard practically devouring Bandelier's highly romanticized novel set in Frijoles Canyon in the 1300s.

21

. . . .

FEELING REFRESHED AFTER TWO DAYS OFF, LULI walked to the gallery as usual on Thursday morning. She was unlocking the door when she heard footsteps and turned to see four huge men, three of them black, standing behind her. They looked like linebackers, not antiques customers. Luli's heart began to pound. Were they going to rob her? Should she run? Then she noticed they were all dressed alike in dark-colored uniforms. The only Anglo was Mr. Stripey, the man she'd seen standing across the street from the store, the man who had been following her, the guy who always wore a striped shirt. Now he was wearing a uniform with a government agency patch on it that said ICE. He was holding a sheet of paper.

"We have a search warrant," he said gruffly. He and the others flashed badges. The Anglo shoved the paper into Luli's face.

She nearly fainted. "What? A search warrant for what?"

He rattled the document. "Open up the store. Now."

She began to tremble. "I think I need to read this first." She took the paper and tried to make out the small print, but her hand was shaking so badly all she could determine was that the warrant was from the US Federal District Court, and Beto's name was on it.

"I . . . I need to call my boss," she stammered, doing her best to think clearly.

"No, you don't," said the Anglo.

"You won't find him, anyway," one of the other men said.

"Yeah, if we can't find him, you can't either," said another.

The Anglo shot his colleagues an angry look. "Shut up," he ordered.

Inside the store, the men fanned out examining everything. The Anglo stopped at the locked door to Beto's studio. "Gimme the key," he demanded.

"I don't have it," Luli said.

He glowered at her. "Give it to me or I'll add obstructing justice to the other charges against you."

Summoning courage from somewhere, Luli glared right back at him. "I have never had a key to that room," she said tersely. "What charges against me?"

The Anglo didn't reply.

"I'm calling a lawyer. I have no idea what's going on, and I have a right to know."

As flustered as she was, she thought of Sammy Pacheco. She remembered he was a partner in one of the most prestigious law firms in Santa Fe, but she didn't remember which one. She used the store phone to call the Alires.

"Rosealba? This is Luli. I'm at Beto's store. It's full of cops. Except they're acting more like thugs. They have a search warrant. Can you give me Sammy's number? I need him to come immediately."

"M'ija," Rosealba said, "I call him for you. Meantime, don't you say nothing to them cops."

"Believe me, I won't."

The minute she put down the phone, the Anglo started firing questions at her: where was Beto, where did he hide the key to the back room, did he have a storage locker, did she have a storage locker, and so forth.

Luli folded her arms across her chest and sat down in one of the upholstered chairs. "I'm not saying another word until my attorney gets here."

The Anglo's face reddened. He ordered one of the linebacker cops to break down the door to the studio. Before Luli could ask on whose authority, there was a loud crash and the sound of splintering wood. The cop had broken it open with one swift kick. The men filed into Beto's workroom.

Luli got up to answer a rap at the door when the Anglo cop brushed past her and flung it open himself. "Yeah?" he said to a young man dressed in a sport coat and tie.

Sammy Pacheco introduced himself. "I'm from the Hammerstein Kennedy Pacheco firm. I'm representing Mrs. Luli Russell."

The federales spent three hours examining everything in the store. At one point, Mr. Stripey appeared out of the back room triumphantly waving a clear plastic baggie of greenish-brown leaves. "Now we can nail the slippery son of a bitch on drug charges, too."

Upset as she was, it was all Luli could do not to burst out laughing as she watched the cop label Beto's yerba mate "evidence."

The burly officers began to carry stock out of the store, but Sammy Pacheco stopped them. "I'll need an inventory list of the things you're taking. Luli, please write down each item, describe its condition, and the name of the officer carrying it. Bear in mind, gentlemen, you're personally responsible for any damage to Mr. Colilla's property."

Warily, the men loaded the confiscated goods into a huge blue Sequoia parked across the street, its roof bristling with antennae like a giant insect.

Sammy asked the Anglo cop to sign Luli's list. His signature was an angry scrawl. When the federales finished, Mr. Stripey ordered Sammy and Luli out, padlocked the store, and strung yellow crime scene tape across it. They drove off with a screech of tires, the Sequoia lurching as it hopped a curb.

"Let's go have a cup of coffee somewhere," Sammy said. They walked to Downtown Subscription and sat outside at a table far from other customers. Luli was still shaking; she had to hold her coffee mug with both hands.

"You don't have anything to worry about. These guys were just trying to scare you."

"Well, they did a damn good job of it, but I have no idea of what they were after," Luli said. "If there's anything funny going on, I wouldn't know about it. I've only worked there for a couple of months. Why are Immigration and Customs feds after Beto? He told me he had permanent resident status."

"That may be true. But judging from the search warrant, this isn't about immigration. They claim he's a big time pre-Columbian art trafficker, and they're angry as can be because he has given them the slip. I have an old squeeze who works for the FBI in Albuquerque. Maybe I can torture some info out of her."

Luli felt comfortable with Sammy, and she knew the Alires were pleased with his handling of the insurance case when Bea and Joe were killed, but she thought she could be in deep trouble. It seemed wise to check his bonafides. Her brother Bart's best friend was a law professor at the University of Wisconsin. He did some research before he called Luli.

"I'm confident he'll do an excellent job for you," he assured her. "Harvard Law doesn't graduate bozos. Nor do Supreme Court justices hire incompetent clerks. He's barely thirty-five, but he has plenty of experience with the federal courts, and he's well regarded by the local judges. He and I agree the charges against you are baseless. They're simply trying to intimidate you."

But Luli was concerned. "How can I afford him—or any lawyer for that matter?" she asked Bart.

"Sammy hasn't told you?"

"Told me what?"

"His firm is taking on your case pro bono. His partners are former Legal Aid lawyers, and they're not big fans of ICE."

The following week, Sammy told her he had indeed gotten some interesting information out of his former girlfriend. "Let's have lunch," he suggested. "Have you ever been to Carlos' Gospel Café? Delicious soups and sandwiches."

"So was there anything illegal in the shop or Beto's studio?" Luli asked over a bowl of tomato basil soup. "Apart from the big bag of mysterious leaves that are surely dangerous drugs?"

"The entire federal court got a huge laugh out of that, especially the presiding judge's clerk. He's from Uruguay. He knew right away it was yerba mate, not dope. The other thing they found that got ICE all excited was a storage jar. They thought it was a museum-quality Nazca pot from Peru, like a thousand years old or something. It turned out to be Shipibo, circa 1985, from the Peruvian jungle. It didn't even belong to Beto; he was repairing a crack in it for a client."

"I wouldn't know the difference myself."

"The federal prosecutor knows you're not bluffing about having no idea what your boss was up to, or what was in the packages delivered to the shop. They've dropped all charges against you. But they're still going after Beto.

"My FBI friend says the real issue is some problem with an antique writing desk he recently sold an ambassador to

Bolivia for big bucks. The ambassador donated it to the San Antonio Museum of Art, where he found out that it was a fake. Well, the box itself was antique, but the decoration was new. When the curator broke the bad news to the donor, he hit the roof. He fancies himself an expert on Spanish Colonial art and over the years he has made many significant donations to the museum, including other pricey artifacts he bought from Beto. Now all his donations—and the major tax breaks he got for them—are in doubt. His pride is wounded, he's likely to be in debt to the IRS, he's on a rampage to get Beto, and he's calling in all his chips in Washington."

"I remember that box," Luli said quietly. "It was beautiful."

22

ALTHOUGH THE CHARGES AGAINST HER WERE DIS-
missed and her record expunged, the experience left Luli
traumatized. She couldn't sleep, her stomach was upset, and
now that the gallery was closed, she was jobless again, more
penniless and worried than ever. The rent from the Fish
Creek cottage would keep her and the kids going for a bit
longer, but it would soon be gone. Nobody rented a place in
Door County after Labor Day, certainly not a high priced
one like theirs.

Rosealba noticed that Luli was unusually pale and had
bags under her eyes. "What's the matter, m'ija?"

"I'm not sleeping," Luli confessed. "I keep tossing and
turning and having nightmares about those cops bust-
ing down my door. I see that Anglo cop yelling in my face,
accusing me of all sorts of crimes. Me—President of the
Sodality of Our Lady Queen of Heaven twice in a row." She
laughed. "Seriously, though, I've never been mixed up with
anything crooked in my life."

"If you want, Basura can come and stay with you at
night; he can protect you from them bad hombres."

Luli tried it for a few nights. She loved the big, shaggy dog, but he, too, was a restless sleeper, getting up at all hours, pacing the house, the tags on his collar clanging loudly when he shook himself. She gave him back to the Alires. "I'm fine," she said.

But she wasn't fine.

That night, she woke up from yet another nightmare. The cop in the striped shirt jumped her from behind as she put a key in the lock to Beto's store. He handcuffed her, and told her she'd never see her family again. She knew it was all a bad dream, but tears blurred her vision and she began to sob. A pain in her abdomen made her double up. Bile rose in her throat. She got out of bed, but her condition only got worse. She was shivering; her skin was clammy. The tremor in her hands was uncontrollable. The stomach cramps became more acute and spread through her entire body. Her head spun. She couldn't focus. She couldn't breathe. The walls began to cave in on her. Was this a heart attack? A stroke? Appendicitis? Somehow she got into the Ford and drove to the emergency room.

The minute she walked into the hospital, she knew she'd made a mistake. Pale, dazed people, some groaning loudly, many of them bloodied, filled all the chairs in the waiting room. Luli leaned up against a wall until an able looking man insisted she take his seat. In a semi-conscious state, she collapsed into the chair. Anxious young women tried to comfort screaming babies. A man in work clothes paced the hallway hunched over, clutching a clumsily bandaged arm. A teenage boy that someone had used as a punching bag sat on the floor in a daze, his face swollen and purple, his hands lacerated. She closed her eyes and tried to tune out the horrors around her. For several hours, sounds came in and out of her head like waves crashing violently on a rocky beach. Finally, a nurse gently woke her and asked what the problem was. Luli opened her eyes. "Where am I?" she asked.

"You're in the emergency room at St. Vincent's Hospital. In Santa Fe. Can you tell me what's wrong?"

Luli shook her head as if to dispel her confusion. Again the nurse asked what the problem was. Finally, she understood. "I . . . I think I need to talk to somebody." Miraculously, she recalled the name of the Alire's niece. "Is Dr. Inés Pacheco on duty?" she asked in a tiny, quavering voice.

After what seemed like another eon, the nurse returned and took Luli gently by the arm. The next thing she knew, she was sitting in Dr. Pacheco's office, with a blanket wrapped around her shoulders. The doctor sat facing her. She leaned forward and held Luli's trembling hands. "Tell me what's going on."

In a flood of tears, Luli stammered out a litany of woes: the terrifying raid on Beto's shop, the menacing federales, the nightmares—all of this on top of her husband's betrayal, worries about her kids, the loss of her home, her financial situation, her decision to leave Green Bay, her inability to find a job in Santa Fe. "I'm so embarrassed," she kept repeating. "How did I get myself into such a mess?"

Dr. Pacheco's voice was soothing. "None of this is your fault. Trust me. What happened to you can and does happen to a lot of people, especially to a lot of women suddenly on their own. I know it looks hopeless right now. But you're a survivor. Even if you feel awful, things will get better. You're strong, your kids love you, you're intelligent, you have lots going for you.

"I don't know if this is helpful, but I've been in your shoes. I foolishly got married right after high school and had two kids in three years. I worked nights as a nurse's aide to put my husband through college, then law school. For seven years, I did all the housework, all the kid care, sleeping whenever I could, which was never enough. A month after he passed the bar exam, he dumped me and our kids, and moved out of state with his new girlfriend. Never paid a dime of child support."

Luli looked up through a wash of tears. "How on earth did you become a doctor?"

Dr. Pacheco smiled. "I had lots of support. You will, too. You're not in this alone. Tell you what. I have a psychiatrist friend who would be much more helpful to you than me— Dr. Rachel Hirsch. She's terrific. She got me through the most hopeless, messiest part of my situation. I credit her with saving my life, in fact. Here's her number."

Dr. Pacheco scribbled the information on a piece of paper and gave it to Luli. "I'll be right back," she said.

When she returned, she gave Luli a small handful of pills and a paper cup of water. "What you've had is an anxiety attack. A perfectly normal response to being overwhelmed by unpleasant, scary circumstances. These will help you get some rest. And here's a prescription for more. Please call Dr. Hirsch in the morning. She's expecting to hear from you."

"This is more than kind of you, but I can't afford a psychiatrist." Luli sniffled and blew her nose on a tissue. "Don't they charge two hundred dollars an hour?"

"Don't worry about it. You and Dr. Hirsch can work something out. I've also called my aunt and uncle. They're coming right now to pick you up."

The news sent Luli into another crying jag. "I don't want to be a burden to them. They've had way too many tragedies of their own to deal with. They don't need mine, too. And they're taking care of Flip. They've already been so generous to me. They barely know me."

"Luli, they think the world of you, and they're happy to help. That's the kind of people they are. Believe me, you're no burden to them whatsoever."

Luli met Dr. Hirsch in her downtown office the following day. "I can't pay you much," she said apologetically "But I could clean your house or office for you."

"I'm sure we can figure out a deal. I love trading. Don't fret about it," the doctor said.

Luli realized immediately Dr. Hirsch was easy to talk to, trustworthy, thoughtful, experienced. She didn't hold back her opinions either.

"Luli, everything you've told me about Herb convinces me he's a total shit."

Dr. Hirsch smiled as Luli's chin hit the floor.

"Shocked? I bet in Green Bay, women don't talk like that about their husbands—even their exes. But I make it a habit to say what I think and I think he's an asshole."

"Well, yes, I guess he is," Luli admitted.

"Think about it. Don't make excuses for him. Get mad! Last week you told me what he gave you for your twenty fifth wedding anniversary, a gold-plated Green Bay Packer football key chain."

"Yeah. The gold plating wore off in a couple of weeks. It was some kind of brass underneath."

"And don't forget what he gave you for your fiftieth birthday."

"I'll never forget that," she said.

Late that night, Luli heard a scratching on her bedroom screen and sat up, her heart drumming so fast she thought it would break through the wall of her chest. The scratching came again. This was no bad dream; something or someone was at her window.

"Pssst, Señora Luli. Is me, Kiko, the friend of Beto who play the guitarra. Beto ask me to give you the money he owe you."

Luli was half-asleep, but she remembered the curly-haired young man, the gypsy.

"I'll meet you at the back door, Kiko." As she walked into the kitchen and turned on the dim light above the stove, she wondered if she was doing something stupid. Should she let him in? He seemed trustworthy, but maybe all the Chileans were involved in whatever had gotten Beto into trouble with the law. She opened the door a crack. Kiko made no move to come in, but stretched out a fistful of hundred dollar bills. "Is $1,000 for you," he said in a low voice.

Luli didn't take the money. "He doesn't owe me that much, not even half that."

"Beto say to tell you he so, so sorry for all the problems he make for you. Take it. Please."

Luli wanted to ask if Beto was all right, but the second she accepted the bills, Kiko disappeared back into the darkness.

She told no one about the money. It seemed safer that way.

23

. . . .

ALTHOUGH THE CASH GAVE HER A BIT OF A CUSHION, it was time to look for a new job. She polished her shoes and her résumé, glossing over the job with Beto. If someone asked why she'd left his employ, she'd say he decided to close the gallery and return to Chile. Not every prospective employer in town was aware of the raid on his store.

Now that the Santa Fe tourist season was about to end, there were even fewer listings in the want ads. On her third day of making the rounds of stores, hotels, and restaurants in unusually hot early fall weather, she was home by three, lying on the couch with her sore feet up and her eyes closed. Soon she heard the low rumble of Rosealba's old Chevy and Basura's loud, excited barks. She got up, straightened out her skirt, tucked her blouse in, slipped her flats back on her painfully swollen feet, and crossed the driveway to the Alire's house.

Rosealba looked up when Luli approached. "How'd it go today, niña?"

"More of the same. It's hopeless. But I've got an idea I'd like your opinion on."

"Sure. Come inside. How about some agua de piña? Pineapple juice. I make it this morning."

"You're on. It sounds delicious—¡sabroso!"

They sat down at the kitchen table, moisture from the frosty glasses of golden juice puddling on the red oilcloth.

Luli leaned her chin on her palm. "Can you help me find a housecleaning job?"

Rosealba looked at her in surprise.

"Really. I'm good. I've always cleaned my own house, I'm a total neatnik, I'm thorough, I won't steal the silverware, and God knows, I need the money."

"But you've got a college degree, m'ija."

"That and a dollar won't buy me a cup of coffee in this town."

"Oh, isn't that true? I hear people pay four dollars for a coffee at that Star Wars place or whatever it's called—the café in De Vargas Mall. Can you believe it?"

"Yes. Nothing's cheap in Santa Fe, except the wages. So what do you think? Do you know of any housecleaning jobs?"

Rosealba picked up one of Luli's hands, turned it over and rubbed her fingers against its soft palm. Then she stroked Luli's cheek. It was like being caressed by a piece of sandpaper.

"This is what them cleaners do to your skin," she sighed. "My hands are like old leather, like carne seca."

"Isn't that why God made rubber gloves and lotion?"

"They help some, but sooner or later, your skin dries out and cracks, even if you use gloves and put Bag Balm on it every night."

"Bag Balm? What's that?"

"It's the stuff farmers put on their cows' udders. It's almost pure lanolin. But even that's not enough. You can't be serious about house cleaning, m'ija. It's awful hard work, especially if you're not used to it."

"I am totally serious. And I'm not afraid of hard work."

Rosealba thought for a minute. "Well, I know of one job, but the lady is very picky, and she don't pay so much."

"How much?"

"Ten dollars an hour. My other ladies pay me fifteen. That's why I quit her. Other people did too. She's very fussy, very strict. She's pushy, but she don't want to pay you nothing. Many times, she say she have no money, she pay you later. You have to make another trip to her house for what she owe you."

"Even ten dollars sounds good at this point. The galleries only pay about $7 starting. No benefits, of course."

"This work never have no benefits. I pay my own social security."

"Tell me more about this lady."

Luli, dressed in her oldest but neatly pressed jeans and a clean work shirt, accompanied Rosealba to the Stoss residence on Upper Canyon Road for an introduction.

"Don't tell her I have a college degree," Luli whispered as they approached the back door with the bucket of cleaning supplies Rosealba suggested she buy.

"When I call to tell her about you, I say you're my cousin," Rosealba said, tittering like a schoolgirl. "You know, we're both related to Adam and Eve, no?"

Mrs. Stoss was about the same age as Luli and Rosealba. She was petite, carefully made up and coiffed, smartly dressed in crisp beige linen pants and a pastel patterned silk blouse, with a lightweight alpaca sweater draped over her narrow shoulders. She pursed her lips tightly in an approximation of a smile when Rosealba introduced her cousin, but didn't offer to shake the hand Luli extended.

"I expect honesty, thoroughness, diligence, dependability, and I want things done the way I tell you to do them. Understood?"

Luli nodded.

"You're Rosealba's cousin?" Mrs. Stoss raised her carefully shaped eyebrows and skeptically compared the two women—one short, with a round face, dark hair and dark skin, the other pale, tall, and blonde.

Luli smiled. "We're related through Adam."

"My husband, Adán," Rosealba chimed in. "That's Spanish for 'Adam.' I have to go or I be late for my job. I pick you up at four," she said and went back to her car.

Mrs. Stoss led Luli into the foyer. "You can start with the downstairs bathroom. Now, what was your name again?"

"I'm Mrs. Russell, Mrs. Luli Russell."

"Hmmmm, that's not a Spanish name, is it? Well, Luli, I'm sure we're going to get along splendidly. The pay is $8 an hour, and I expect you to put in full hours."

Luli hesitated, then said: "I understand the pay is $10 an hour. I can't do the job for any less. Of course I'll give you your money's worth."

Mrs. Stoss frowned. "Oh, all right, fine. $10 it is. I'll see to it that you earn it."

With Rosealba's help, Luli soon found several other house-cleaning jobs: a middle-aged couple who owned a Canyon Road gallery; a single woman who taught English at St. John's College; and a young man who didn't seem to do much of anything. The Oglethorpes, were nice enough, but they were both chain-smokers. The stench of cigarettes gagged her every time she opened the door to their John Gaw Meem adobe off Camino del Monte Sol. The smoke had yellowed the once white walls, the thick cotton curtains, and the upholstered furniture to the point where the house would never look or smell clean ever again in spite of Luli's most heroic efforts.

Jasper Nunnally was a gawky, surly young man the age of Luli's twin sons. He was what they would label "a slacker"—or maybe even "a loser." He lived alone in a spacious town house in a neighborhood northwest of the Plaza. It was cluttered with all sorts of electronic equipment, computers, and sports gear. When he wasn't blankly staring at Luli as she attempted to create some semblance of cleanliness in his lair, Jasper slept a lot. The odor of marijuana hung in the air. He paid her in cash, and often had nothing smaller than a hundred dollar bill.

Alice McCready, the English professor, was the most pleasant of Luli's clients, a tidy housekeeper. Cleaning her house was a snap, except for the hair from her seven cats, which left Luli with swollen eyes, a stuffed up nose, and itchy skin.

Luli's children knew their mother was making a living at what Flip termed "domicile maintenance," and it pained them. "It's only temporary," she told them when they called. "And the money is better than I could make working a so-called white collar job."

"But Mom," Jenna whined. "Like, what am I going to tell my friends? 'My mother's in Santa Fe scrubbing toilets for rich people?' Which is what I thought we were before Daddy Dearest absconded with the family fortune?"

"Jenna, we were never rich. We held our own. Frankly, I don't care what you tell your friends. Make up something juicy. Tell them I'm living off a rich Santa Fe boy-toy. With any kind of luck, the gossip will get back to your father."

"MOM!"

"I'm looking for something better, and trying to decide on my next move. Give me a break."

"Well, but we're worried about you. Isn't it, like, really hard work?"

Tucking the telephone between her ear and her shoulder, she inspected her hands. After only two weeks on the job, her nails were broken off down to the nubbins. Her skin was cracked like old majolica. "It's working out, dear heart. I'm getting in really good shape. I'm almost down a size. No more thunder thighs and jelly belly for your ol' middle-aged mom. People pay good money to go to a gym and spend hours at torture machines for this kind of conditioning. I, on the other hand, get paid for my workout. Such a deal!"

Luli and Rosealba often shared rides to their jobs. In a city the size of Santa Fe, the houses they cleaned were never far apart. They got together after work to share a soft drink and exchange news, or chitchat about their clients. Mrs. Stoss, for whom Luli worked two mornings a week, provided the most entertainment.

"She has me iron her husband's swimsuit. Can you believe it?" Luli giggled.

"His swimsuit? ¡Híjole! That's crazy."

"Yeah, and his underwear."

"Well, I suppose boxer shorts could come out kinda wrinkly if you leave 'em in the dryer too long."

Luli laughed. "No—she has me iron his Jockeys."

"Eeee! You're kidding."

"Little ones. The skimpy kind. Red, blue, black, striped. That's not even the weird part. . . . "

"Ooooh, tell me!"

"They're numbered."

Rosealba wrinkled up her face. "¿Cómo?"

"One through seven, for each day of the week. So he wears them out evenly, I guess."

"I'll have to tell Danny that one. He won't believe it."

They snickered like teenagers.

"Careful—he might have you ironing his Jockeys next."

"No chance. He always do his own laundry."

Sometimes Flip joined them for their afternoon kaffee-klatsch. Wearing a neat little smile, he'd sip a cool club soda while he listened to the women discuss their clients' idiosyncrasies.

"This is so fascinating," he said as the trio sat outside under Rosealba's arbor. "I've only heard the other side of the story—my mother and later, my wife complaining about their servants. They spent a great deal of time nattering on about the poor souls—how this maid was lazy, that one surly, they were using my mother's Shalimar on the sly, sneaking nips of sherry, pinching the flatware, having dalliances with the houseboy or the chauffeur."

The women exchanged a quizzical look.

"Maids?" Luli asked.

Flip grinned shyly and took another sip. "That was in another life, of course."

24

· · · · · · ·

A WEEK LATER, ROSEALBA AND LULI SAT BY THEM-
selves in the Alire's back yard. "I haven't seen Flip since
Friday," Luli mentioned. "I went over last night to read to
him, and he didn't answer the door. It was a little late, so I
thought maybe he was sleeping."

"I haven't seen him either. I don't think he went to work
this morning, I'm afraid he's drinking again."

Luli groaned. "What about his family, Rosealba? He
seems to come from money. Could we contact them? To
find him a good rehab program?"

"We only talk about family once, right after he come
to live here. It was obviously a sore point. He says he don't
have no family. What he really said was 'I had a family, but
I lost them all. End of subject.' I didn't mention it again. I'm
awful worried about him. Last night, when Danny went to
check on him, he said he didn't want no supper or nothing.
He told Danny he was 'indisposed,' whatever that means.
Danny thought he smelled whiskey, so maybe Flip's dinner
was coming out of a bottle."

"Oh God. I'll go pay him a visit."

"Tell him dinner tonight is lamb chops, from Adán's brother's ranch in Santa Rosa. Your come too, Luli. Flip likes lamb. Be sure he knows I got some mint jelly to go with it. Can you believe it? He eats his lamb with jelly. But if he's not up to a regular meal, I'll make him some atole instead. If he's been drinking, it would be easier on his stomach."

"What's atole?"

"It's like Cream of Wheat, but made out of cornmeal. I'll put lots of honey in it and a dash of cinnamon. My mother use to make it for my dad when he go on a borrachera, a drunk."

The door to Flip's house was open a crack. Luli knocked, and when there was no answer, she rapped again with her knuckles. A moan came from the bedroom. "Flip?" she called out. "It's Luli. Are you all right?"

She heard another groan. "I'm coming in. I need to see how you're doing."

The elderly man was in bed, lying on his side, his skin the pale yellow of a dried apple. A bloody stream flowed out of his mouth onto the pillow. He opened his eyes and smiled faintly at Luli. "Oops, fell off the wagon," he said in a shaky voice.

She noticed an empty whiskey bottle on the floor by his bed. "I'll go for help." She ran to the Alire's. In minutes, an ambulance siren wailed up the hill, growing louder as it approached the compound.

25

· · · · · · ·

AT THE HOSPITAL, ONCE FLIP HAD BEEN STABILIZED, they met with Dr. Pacheco.

"It's nice to see you, Luli. How are you?"

"I'm doing great, thanks to you and Dr. Hirsch. She's wonderful. I can't thank you enough for putting me together with her."

"I'm pleased. By chance, are you related to Mr. Phillips?"

"No."

Adán sat resting his forearms on his knees as he twirled his baseball cap in his callused hands. "We're all the family he's got—here at least. He says he doesn't have family any more. He lost 'em somehow, and he doesn't want to talk about it. We've been taking care of him for the last six months. Your sister, the one who works in the Social Security office, helped him sign up for the disability. He lives in Antonio's casita behind us. Rosealba and me and Luli—she lives next door—we look after him. When he's feeling well enough, he sells papers downtown, gives us most of what he makes to help pay for his food. He barely eats."

"You Alires and your strays," Ines smiled. "You are the most generous people I know. Well, I guess we put him down as indigent. He must be old enough to be eligible for Medicare."

"He told us he was born in 1928, so he must be somewhere in his mid-seventies," Rosealba said.

"You do realize he's in pretty rough shape?" Dr. Pacheco said with a long face.

Rosealba, Luli, and Adán nodded.

"He has esophageal bleeding and his liver's shot. End-stage alcoholism. If he makes it out of here this time, you absolutely have to keep him from drinking. Even if he does stay away from alcohol, he's not a candidate for a liver transplant. He has congestive heart failure. Frankly, he's not long for this world."

"I think we know that," Luli said. "My dad drank himself to death. I've been down this road before."

"So have I," Rosealba said.

Adán squeezed his wife's knee. "We'll look after him as best we can."

"You're saints," Dr. Pacheco said. "Call on me anytime. Here's my cell phone number."

Flip was in the hospital for several days, then went home to his little house. The Alires and Luli took turns bringing him mild, nourishing food, sitting with him to make sure he ate at least something. Although he had improved slightly, he was bone thin. His skin remained the dim gold of a faded sunflower. He couldn't take more than a few steps at a time, shuffling from his bed to the bathroom, then back to bed. After a week of rest, however, he was able to make his way slowly to the armchair in his living room and sit upright for longer and longer intervals.

Luli resumed reading to him. After she finished a Bob Shacochis short story set in the Caribbean, Flip chuckled at the farcical ending. "Sounds just like life in Sainte Foi," he said.

"You've been there, I take it?"

"For several generations, my family has had a house there, right on the Baie de Ste. Foi. A wonderful, pale blue cottage surrounded by a veranda—La Maison Azure. Maybe we still have it—I don't know. I love the islands. There's no color like the turquoise of the Caribbean on a sun-drenched day, the golden beaches, the intensely green palms. And the people—they have an admirable attitude toward life. 'Pas de problèmes—No worries, mon', about sums up their philosophy. Of course they have the same worries and torments and preoccupations as people everywhere. But they believe in being sanguine, optimistic, enjoying life to its maximum. I've always envied them that."

Flip grew thoughtful. Then he looked up at Luli with his watery blue eyes. "How are you?"

"I'm OK, Flip. Thanks for asking."

"No, I mean, are you getting along well here in Santa Fe?"

"I am. Thanks to the Alires and their amazing network of family and friends, I'm starting to feel at home. I love my adobe casa. The weather's glorious and mild, the pace is measured, and people are generally kind to one another.

185

Santa Fe's a special place. There's history and depth and character here. It's not the plastic franchised sprawl so much of our country has become—the type of soulless 'development' people like my ex-husband build. Even Cerrillos Road still has its own funky shops and homey little eateries, among the chain motels, fast food joints, and big box stores."

"Are you still cleaning houses?"

"Yes. It's very hard work, but I've toughened up. I'm making twice what I would in a gallery. I'm thinking of taking accounting and computer classes at the Community College, if I can come up with the tuition."

"Splendid idea. You hold a college degree already, don't you?"

"Yes, but it's in education—nearly useless unless you want to teach, and I don't. I've always been good at numbers. Actually, for years, I did my husband's books until he fired me. I guess because he didn't want me to know he was losing so much money, dipping into our savings, and mortgaging us to the hilt. I know accounting basics. In a year or so, I should be able to find a good job. Eventually, I'd like to set up my own bookkeeping service."

"Your family?"

"My family's bouncing back. Scripps found scholarships for my youngest, so she can start college in January. Allie got her Ph.D. in psychology in the spring and has a temp job in a Chicago hospital this fall. My twin sons have managed to stay in school. They're getting financial help from the athletic program and work part-time in the cafeteria. I feel horrible about not being able to pay for their college education. I thought my husband and I had put away enough money. But since the louse absconded with everything, we're destitute." Her face shattered like windshield glass, and she burst into tears.

Flip handed her a tissue from a box on the side table.

"I apologize. You don't need to hear about my sorry circumstances."

"My dear, you have absolutely nothing to be ashamed of. I have all the admiration in the world for you. You're a strong, creative, intelligent, hard-working woman who's loyal to her children. They'll be enriched by the experience. Working their way through college isn't the worst that can happen to them. Your husband's a scoundrel. I know all about being a perfidious husband and father. That's how I lost my own family. Mark my words—he'll come to regret his selfishness, his faiblesse, and his stupidity. He will rue his indiscretions."

"Oh, Flip," she sniffled. "Don't you think you could mend fences with your family? Maybe they can pardon you for whatever happened?"

He shook his head. He stared despondently at the faded, worn carpet at his feet. "It's much too late, my dear. Especially now that I'm a complete wreck of a human being, surely living out my last days. I could never make up for the wretched way in which I abandoned them, my son, in particular."

"Are you sure, Flip? People do forgive one another, you know. Maybe it's not as hopeless as you think."

"Oh, yes it is," he said firmly. Then he looked up at her with rheumy eyes. He took a deep breath. "I have something I want you to do for me."

"I'm happy to help however I can."

"It's a big something. Don't say yes until you've heard me out and thought through my proposal."

"Try me."

He sighed, reached into his pocket, and brought out a delicate gold chain with an engraved gold coin pendant. He studied the necklace for a long time, then handed it to Luli. "My younger son, Henri, gave this to me for my birthday. He found it on the beach in Sainte Foi. It was his prize possession."

She held the coin in her palm. "It's beautiful, Flip. What is it?"

"It's an eight escudos cob, from the Seville mint, 1663–1666, worth at least $3,000 in today's market, I'd think. Somehow, in the mayhem of my many years of drunken carousing, I managed to hang onto this. Henri . . . he died a year after he gave it to me, when he was ten . . ."

"Oh, I'm so sorry. There can be no greater loss than to lose a child. I can't imagine it." She saw Flip's eyes were clouded with tears. "What a wonderful keepsake. Something special to remember him by."

"I collected cobs," Flip said, dabbing at his eyes with a tissue.

"What are cobs?" Luli asked. "I've never heard that term before—except for corn, and race horses."

"The word 'cob' originally meant a lump of something, such as a piece of coal. The first coins in the Spanish Americas were irregular planchets of silver or gold struck by hand in mints set up in the four viceroyalties.

"These were the original pieces of eight or divisions thereof that bore the King's name or coat of arms as well as the mint that made them or the assayer's mark. If the eight real piece weighed too much, or someone wanted less than a full piece of eight, a 'bit' was cut off. A fourth of the circle was two bits."

"Like our quarters?"

"Yes. That's where the term comes from. These Spanish dollars were used throughout the world and were legal currency in the U.S. until 1858. This is why the New York Stock Exchange used to halve stock quotations down to quarters and eighths. The system was based on eighths, not decimals."

"Fascinating, Flip. Obviously, you've studied these."

"Yes. I had a large, serious collection of Spanish Colonial cobs from all over the Americas and Spain. Like my father before me, I was a Wall Street stockbroker and very successful at it. Collecting coins was my passion. Henri knew I'd be thrilled to add this to my holdings, and I absolutely was. It was the most wonderful present anyone ever gave me. After he died, I left Ste. Foi. This was all I took. That was more than thirty years ago."

Luli reached for Flip's skeletal hand and held it.

He looked up and brightened. "Are you ready to entertain my proposal?"

"Sure, I guess so."

"I want you to retrieve my collection from Sainte Foi. I want to sell it, do some good with the proceeds before I forsake this vale of tears. Many people have been kind to me through the years—rehab programs around the country that tried to save my sorry soul, St. Elizabeth's Shelter here in Santa Fe, the Alires, you, Dr. Pacheco and her staff. I want to demonstrate my appreciation for your kindness to this useless old sot. My colleagues—my fellow drunks—and I have done so much harm to our families, our communities, ourselves. I'm not long for this world, nor am I in any condition to make the trip myself."

"What about your family?"

"Before I departed like a tosspot banshee in a howling gale, I sold my portfolio. I put the proceeds in trust for my surviving son, Jean-Luc. My ex-wife was gone. She'd decamped with a tennis pro. When the boys were five and seven, we divorced. Subsequently, she died in a car accident in Switzerland—she was probably driving drunk."

"This is extraordinarily generous of you, but I don't see how I could do it. I don't have the money for a trip. I have to keep working."

"That's where this coin comes in, my dear. It will provide you with more than enough for your travel to Ste. Foi, pay for your lodging, and make up for your lost income."

Luli was astonished. "You'd sell this? But it was your son's gift. You just told me how much it means to you."

"Actually, I wouldn't quite sell it. I'd ask a top-notch coin dealer to hold it for me, one who's bound to salivate when he hears what else is in the collection. If he has been in the trade for a while, he'll have heard of me and my collection—such as the dozen grade 1 gold escudos said to have come from the Atocha shipwreck of 1622. I scooped those right up when they came on the market.

"My mind is a Swiss cheese at this point. I can't remember an event five minutes after it happens. But curiously, my long-term memory still enables me to recall the most valuable of my coins. We'll have the dealer keep my escudo as collateral, providing us the wherewithal for you to travel in exchange for giving him first option on the entire hoard. The price of gold is more than fifty times what it was in the sixties, so I'd surmise the bullion value alone is easily a million dollars. I had 1,238 gold cobs from various mints, in addition to several hundred silver cobs, and a few odds and ends, like some Spanish Colonial gold and emerald jewelry my wife missed when she took her leave of us."

Luli had never seen Flip so animated. He was glowing. His wispy white hair, airborne with static in the dry Indian Summer heat, gave him a beatific look. "I'll have to think about it, Flip. It's quite overwhelming."

"Please do. In the meantime, if you can procure me some paper and a pen, I'll begin to make a list of my best coins. I'll also suggest some of the numismatists I used to buy from. With any luck, one or two of them might still be active in the trade. I'll give you directions to the safe where I left the collection, and a key to it. You'll need the key as well as the combination to open the vault. It's in a secret place in the old manse on Ste. Foi; Luc may still own the house. Sainte Foi was where he wanted to be—not in Manhattan or at Andover."

"Wouldn't you like to reconcile with your son?" she asked gently.

Flip's chin rested on his chest. "He surely has no desire to hear from me or of me ever again. There's not a day goes by when I don't yearn for him and wish for his forgiveness. But I'm certain he hates me. After all, I'm responsible for his mother's departure and his brother's death, and I abandoned him."

"Don't you know someone else who could retrieve your collection for you, Flip? Your brother?"

"I'm sure Randolph is dead. He was a dozen years my elder. Probably died of alcoholism himself. It's the family curse. Alas, Luli, there's nobody I trust. No, you're the right person for this job. I know you are."

Luli and the Alires got together over the weekend for Luli's favorite of Rosealba's dishes, enchiladas suizas. During dinner, they discussed Flip's proposal.

"Do you think he's loco?" Luli asked.

"Well, after a lifetime of alcohol abuse, and at his age, I think he's a little off track," Adán said. "But no, I don't think he's completely lost his marbles. For one thing, he showed me the list he's been working on. It's a long one, very detailed, like which coin came from which mint, a date, where it was found, and who he bought it from. He knows a lot about those old coins and the people who buy and sell them."

"Let's say he could get an advance based on the eight escudos he has, and I make the trip, and the collection is still in the safe. Wouldn't somebody accuse me of theft? Or of taking advantage of a sick, old man who's practically on his death bed?"

"Let's talk to Sammy," Roscalba suggested. "He was so wonderful with the insurance companies, and then he help you, Luli, when them cops try to pin something on you. He spend time with us to make our will, ¿verdad, Danny? He explain everything real good, and wouldn't take no money for all his work."

They met with Sammy in his office in a brick Victorian house on Palace Avenue that had been built by a prosperous nineteenth century merchant. Luli was pleased to see him, and thanked him again. She noticed the gentle, respectful, old-fashioned deference he showed his aunt and uncle. His office was like a cozy living room, where they sat in comfortable, Navajo rug patterned furniture. He served them Cokes. Sammy listened thoughtfully as Luli and the Alires took turns telling him about Flip. He asked a number of pertinent questions.

"That's a pretty wild story," he remarked. "My dad told me you'd taken in yet another stray, Aunt Rosealba."

"Two!" Luli said. "I couldn't survive here if it weren't for your family."

Sammy smiled. "Over the years, my aunt and uncle have taken any number of people under their wings. As if having four children of their own weren't enough to deal with. And my cousins were a handful.

"Let's do this. I'll have a talk with Flip, see what his wishes are. Then we can have him evaluated by a psychiatrist. If she gives the nod, and Flip agrees, one of you can be named his executor with Power of Attorney to make decisions for him."

"Couldn't it be all three of us?" Luli asked.

"It's much simpler if it's one person," Sammy said. "Somebody Flip knows and trusts."

"You go ahead, Luli," Adán said. "You understand these things better than us."

PART IV

26

· · · · · · ·

ON A BRIGHT DAY IN SEPTEMBER, LULI PAUSED AT THE top of a narrow staircase leading to the tarmac from the small plane that had ferried her from Puerto Rico to the Caribbean island of Ste. Foi. In spite of the mildly hot, humid day, she was shivering with excitement. Wow! she thought as she surveyed the womb-warm dreamscape laid out before her. Is this for real? Palms swayed in a gentle breeze beneath the brilliant blue sky mottled with cream-puff clouds. At the end of the runway, the sun's glare glinted off a white sand beach that met the smooth, sky-colored ocean. Pelicans winged overhead, looking prehistoric. Now and then a seabird folded its wings and plunged straight down into the water, coming up seconds later with a fish hanging from its beak.

The pilot stood at the bottom of the steps. "Madame, please come down," he said patiently. "I must board my new passengers and take off again in a few minutes."

"Ooops, sorry."

He smiled. "First time here?"

"Yes. I've never been out of the U.S. before. This is so exotic!" She walked down the steps.

"Have a wonderful time," the pilot said.

Luli gingerly made her way into the miniscule airport. She was both thrilled and terrified. If she blinked, would everything disappear? Would she wake up in her adobe in Santa Fe? Or in her bedroom in Green Bay?

Fifty years old and here she was on her own in a foreign country. The island was barely ten miles long, a French protectorate, with French the lingua franca. "Ooooh, la la!" she said under her breath.

As excited as she was about the trip, she was still uneasy about her bizarre mission for Flip. In spite of assurances from him, Sammy, the Alires, and Dr. Hirsch that everything was on the level, she wondered if she should be on Ste. Foi at all.

An official sitting at a desk in a crisp, short-sleeved white uniform shirt held out his hand for her documents. "Bienvenue à Ste. Foi, madame," he said. He stamped her passport and handed it back to her, adding in English, "Enjoy your stay with us."

Luli hoped there would be a taxi or shuttle to take her to the house she'd found searching the Internet on a library computer. As she stood by the luggage carrousel, a smiling, neatly dressed, dark-skinned man walked up to her. "Taxi, madame?" he asked in a lilting English—or was it French?

Not waiting for her answer, he matter-of-factly took her suitcase and wheeled it to the only taxi in sight. Her fellow passengers were met by friends or relatives, who kissed them on both cheeks and took them to waiting cars in the parking lot.

"Where are you staying?" the taxi driver asked as he put her luggage into the trunk and opened the back door for her.

She handed him the sheet of paper she'd printed out from the website that showed a photo of a tiny pink house, complete with driving instructions from the airport.

"I know the place," the driver said. "It's very nice, close to shopping and beaches. Très charmant. Not too priccy. Madame DuFour will take good care of you."

With one hand resting on his driver's side mirror, he made small talk as he piloted her briskly along a narrow road bordered by colorful cottages and small hotels snuggled into tropical foliage.

At first glance, the island reminded her of summertime Door County. People in beach wear meandered aimlessly all over the road, oblivious to traffic, licking ice cream cones, sipping Cokes, stopping in the middle of the street to take snapshots. In the patios of roadside cafes, bordered by flowerboxes of pink and red impatiens, tourists sat at tables under striped umbrellas eating, reading books or newspapers, tapping on laptops, chatting. Nobody was in a hurry to go anywhere or do anything.

Winding in and out of the jumble of jeeps, motor scooters, bicycles, and pedestrians, they drove around a bay, then up a hill and into the driveway of a pink wooden house with white shutters and gingerbread trim on a cliff overlooking a rocky beach. "Et voilà," the driver said. He lugged her suitcase up the stairs to the front door.

A petite older woman, her head haloed in braids, came out of the house. "Bienvenue," she said with a broad smile.

"Merci," Luli replied, hoping she'd remember enough of her two college semesters of French to communicate if her landlady didn't speak English.

The house was exactly what she had hoped for—sunny and clean, with white wicker furniture, a cool tile floor, and a serviceable kitchen. Madame DuFour had left a bowl of fruit on the counter and several bottles of water in the refrigerator. The dining-living room area faced the ocean. To the rear of the house were two comfortable bedrooms. Best of all, a porch ran the width of the cottage, equipped with lawn chairs and a little table, overlooking the Baie de Ste. Foi. Luli knew this was where she'd spend much of her time with her books and watercolors.

In a mixture of English and French, Madame DuFour showed Luli around, then pointed down the road toward the Supermarché, and gave her tips on inexpensive cafés and the most convenient beaches. "You must visit my mother's bakery. We live behind it, if you need me for anything. Her bread is the best French bread you've ever had. She's ninety-three. She bakes two hundred loaves every day in her wood-burning oven. They are all sold before noon."

"Really? She bakes that many loaves of bread? Every day?"

"Sauf les dimanches. Never on Sunday. I forgot to save you a loaf today. But you can buy other bread at the Supermarché."

After Luli settled into the larger bedroom, she walked downhill to the market in search of a few groceries for dinner and the next couple of days. Many of the items in the shop were unfamiliar—some of the tropical fruits, the cheeses, the cold cuts. She bought a package of sliced ham, a few rolls, unsalted butter, two cheeses, several oranges, a bunch of sad-looking and pricey lettuce, grape tomatoes, and—why not—a bottle of French vin rouge.

She was pleased with herself as she successfully communicated with the cashier in French and paid in the unfamiliar Euros she'd traded during her layover in Puerto Rico. Luli took her shopping bags and walked back uphill to her cottage in the dusk.

The breeze coming off the bay was refreshing as she sat at the table outside, enjoying her French picnic dinner, and sipping her wine. The sunset was glorious, a rosy pink that evolved into a deep magenta, then purple before darkness descended. In the clear ocean air, stars emerged like spotlighted actors from a darkened stage. The moon was a faint glow on the eastern horizon. Lights winked from houses and hotels along the far shore.

"I could get used to this," Luli thought. But she wished someone were there to share the beauty of the island with her. Jenna, her future oceanographer, would be thrilled. How could Flip ever walk away from such a lovely place?

First thing in the morning, she strolled to Madame DuFour's house, a simple tin-roofed dwelling behind the bakery exhaling the delicious scent of freshly baked bread.

Madame was hanging up her laundry. "Tout va bien?"

"Très, très bien. Fantastique, merci! I've just run out of my French vocabulary."

Madame laughed. "How can I aid you?"

"I'm looking for a family that lived here for many years, the Phillips."

Madame DuFour frowned. "Ooooh," she said sadly. "Les Phillips. Monsieur Flip and Madame Sylvie?"

Luli nodded.

"Une histoire très tragique. Hélas, they are gone for many years. Their house is very close to yours. It was once the loveliest and most grand maison on the island. But now it is boarded up. Si triste."

"Does anyone from the family still live here?"

"Yes, their son, Jean-Luc. He has the yacht harbor in the Vieille Ville. He is très charmant. You know the family?"

Luli decided it was prudent to say as little as possible about her relationship with Flip. Obviously, something terrible had happened. "I know friends of the family."

Madame looked up the yacht harbor's phone number in the island's thin directory and told her how to find the place.

Before walking back uphill, Luli stopped in at the bakery. She introduced herself to Madame DuFour's mother, an ancient little woman no wider or weightier than a broom handle, brown as her bread, but dusted in white flour. The baker's slender braids crowned her head like her daughter's.

"Bienvenue à nôtre belle isle," she said, whistling words through her few remaining teeth. She deftly lifted a tray of loaves from the oven with sinewy arms as thin as her pains ficelles. Luli bought two. After the slightest of hesitations, she added a chocolate croissant to her string bag.

At the house, she sat on the porch eating the pastry and drinking coffee with ice and milk. What would she say to Jean-Luc? This whole expedition was folly. She'd never done such a thing in her life. Would he think she was a nutcase? Or out to take unfair advantage of his elderly father? Finally, she screwed up her courage and called the yacht harbor. As far as she could understand, the man who answered said Jean-Luc was out on the dock working on a boat engine.

"J'attends, s'il vous plaît," she said, hoping her French was comprehensible.

During the several minutes before Jean-Luc came to the phone, she became increasingly anxious, and nearly hung up.

"Jean-Luc Phillips here. How can I help you?" He had the slightest of French accents.

"I, uh. Hi. My name is Luli Russell. I'm here from the States. I'd like to meet with you for a few minutes, if you don't mind," she stammered.

"Can you tell me what this is about?"

"It's not a sales pitch or anything. It's kind of . . . personal. I think it would be better if we discussed this face to face."

"Ça va," he said. "I'm in the middle of repairing an engine. How about later today, say around five? There's a café across from the main square in the Old Town—the St. Jérôme. Will that work for you?"

"Yes. Thank you. I'll have on a flower-print dress and a straw hat. I'm fifty, with graying blonde hair."

"Moi aussi," Jean-Luc said. "Well, I won't be wearing a dress or a straw hat—a greasy T-shirt and shorts instead. À bientôt, madame."

Luli arrived a few minutes early. First she ordered a coffee, then changed it to lemonade. She was jittery enough already. Jean-Luc arrived a few minutes after five; they spotted each other immediately. He held out his hand, shook hers, and sat down. He examined her with eyes the deep blue of the Baie de Ste. Foi, and seemed to like what he saw, raising his white blond eyebrows approvingly. She could see a strong resemblance to his father—his wispy, snowy hair, a fine aquiline nose, well-defined features that on Flip accentuated his gauntness, but on his son, enhanced his weathered good looks.

She spoke in a rush of words. "As I told you, I'm Luli Russell, from Santa Fe. I'm a friend of your father's."

Jean-Luc grimaced. "So the old bastard's still alive, huh. Like I give a shit. Forgive me—we have some ugly history. I think I'll leave now." He pushed his chair back.

Luli reached across the table. "Please stay and hear me out. I've come a long way to see you. Flip said you had every reason to hate him, and he wasn't sure you'd talk to me. But I had to try."

"You seem like a nice lady. I don't hate my father. But . . ."

"You don't have to explain. Flip's an alcoholic, and alcoholics are very hard on the people around them. My father was one. His drinking did tremendous damage to all of us. Ultimately, it killed him. Your father's in Santa Fe, and he's very ill. He has end stage alcoholism. The doctor says he doesn't have long to live."

"Je suis désolé," Jean-Luc said with a touch of sarcasm in his voice. He folded his arms across his chest. "What does he want from me?"

"Before he dies, he wants to see you and ask for your forgiveness. But he doubts you'll come."

"He's right about that."

"I understand."

"No, you don't!" Jean-Luc said heatedly, his face flushed. "I'm sorry. Too bad you came all this way. Have a nice stay on our island." He got up to leave.

"Please," Luli said. "I brought some papers for you to look at. It's important. Flip was quite certain you wouldn't want to see him. But he'd like to do some good in the world he's about to leave, and he needs your help. Just take a look at the documents—please? He named me the executor of his estate—while he's alive, anyway."

Hesitating, Jean-Luc looked down at Luli. Then he thrust his hand out. "Eh bien, lay 'em on me." He took the envelope. "I can't promise you anything. Forgive me if I'm being rude. If I'd had a mother OR a father growing up, I might be more of a gentleman."

Luli smiled. "Well, at least you listened to me. That was gentlemanly of you."

He shrugged. "Do you need these back?"

"After you read them, we can talk—that is, if you're up for it. I'll be here another six days."

"Where do I find you?"

"I'm at Maribelle DuFour's little pink cottage up the hill from the Supermarché on the left."

"I know where it is," Jean-Luc sighed. "I'll be in touch."

27

· · · · · · ·

DAYS WENT BY WITHOUT A WORD FROM JEAN-LUC.
Luli slipped into a comfortable routine. Early mornings,
she walked downtown for a day old *New York Times* and
fresh bread, then home for a breakfast of café au lait, fruit,
bread, and cheese. She'd paint well into the afternoon, then
put on her swimsuit, grab a towel, and head for one of the
sandy beaches she could reach on foot. She strolled the
shoreline, swam in the clear tepid water, read in the shade
of a sea grape tree, and swam again. When the sun began to
slide toward the horizon, she returned to her cottage. She
was a little lonely, though the island was lovely. Increasingly
she feared her trip had all been for naught. What would she
say to Flip?

On the fifth day, somber clouds moved in. The air grew
still and sticky. She opted to keep working on her latest
watercolor of the bay and go to the beach later if the weather
cleared up. The challenge was to capture the ever-changing
hues of the ocean as the clouds gathered.

She was concentrating so hard that the sound of footsteps made her jump. Jean-Luc climbed up the steps onto
the porch, holding the envelope she'd given him.

"You're still here?" he asked.

"Of course," Luli answered, pulling out a chair for him. "My plane doesn't leave for another two days."

"Jesus. Didn't anybody tell you about the ouragan?"

"What's an ouragan?"

"It's a fucking hurricane! It's headed straight for us. Supposed to hit sometime early tomorrow morning. I can't believe Madame DuFour didn't tell you. Or somebody at the grocery store. Christ!" he scowled.

"Madame's not here. She went to St. Maarten a couple of days ago with her mother for a doctor's appointment. Maybe she mentioned something about a tempête, a storm, but sometimes her English and my French don't fill in all the blanks."

Jean-Luc slapped the envelope down on the glass-topped table. "You can't stay here. This house isn't sturdy enough to withstand hurricane winds. It's too late to catch a plane out. The last ferry left for St. Maarten an hour ago. Goddammit! What am I going to do with you?"

Luli's temper rose. "I can take perfectly good care of myself. I'm not your problem," she said curtly.

Jean-Luc ignored her, got up from his chair, and disappeared around the corner of the house. She could hear him stomping through the underbrush. Below the porch, he opened a creaky door. "Come on down. There's a storm shelter. Probably used to be a cistern. Maybe you can ride out the hurricane here."

Luli walked toward his voice and scrambled down a steep hillside. Beneath the porch, set into the cement-block foundation, was a sturdy-looking, partially open metal door. She heard Jean-Luc inside. As soon as she walked in she started sneezing. "God, it's musty in here."

"True, but this place is probably going to save your life." He stood in the middle of the room, surveying it. "There's a kerosene lantern but no kerosene, candles but no matches . . . oooh, that mattress is skanky. We can drag down a clean one from upstairs." He seemed to be checking off a mental list of the supplies she'd need. "I'll buy you bottled water, at least a case, food that doesn't need cooking—you're not vegan are you?—more candles, matches, a flashlight . . . Ew, not a beautiful toilet . . ." He flushed it. The shallow pool of scummy water in the bowl disappeared and when the tank filled, the water was slightly less dingy. "But it's serviceable. When the lights go off, the pump won't work, so we need to haul in buckets of water for flushing."

Luli was suddenly anxious. She looked around the claustrophobic windowless room that measured twelve feet by fifteen at best, plus the tiny bathroom. At least there was a hole in the door where there must have once been a knob, so she could have fresh air. But the place was awful, grimy, dusty, cluttered with years' worth of cobwebs, dirt, and dead bugs. It stank of mildew and rot.

"How long do these . . . ouragans . . . last?" she asked.

"It varies. Two, three days maybe."

Luli was shocked. She couldn't imagine being immured in that dismal hole by herself for even an hour or two, much less three days.

"We almost never have hurricanes here, but the weather service says this time we're directly in its path. It's huge—the size of the state of Texas— and a category five."

"Meaning what?"

"Winds up to 150 miles an hour, a storm surge of eighteen feet or more, major damage. Hurricane Andrew was a category five. Gotta run. I'll see you soon." He trotted up the slope and sped out of the driveway in his ragtop Jeep.

While Jean-Luc went in search of provisions, Luli did what she could to clean up the space and make it habitable. In less than an hour, he was back with bags of groceries, bottles of kerosene, a case of bottled water, bags of ice, and other supplies he ferried down the hill to the shelter. They dragged the moldy mattress outside, replacing it with one from an upstairs bedroom. A heap of sailing gear occupied one corner. Luli tossed the mildewed sails outside but kept the gaffs and spars on Luc's advice.

"Never can tell when you might need one," he said.

When the space was cleaner and outfitted, Jean-Luc rested his fists on his hips and frowned.

"Sorry I have to leave. We've got to take all our boats out of the water and tow them to the interior of the island. We don't have much time left. The last one to go is mine, and that's where I live.

"I saw a good short-wave radio upstairs and several flashlights. I bought you lots of batteries. You should be all set. I'll check in on you when it's over. Do not even dream of going out until I come for you. Whole trees will be flying around. A tin roof in that kind of wind can cut you in half. You're high enough up the cliff that the surge won't drown you, but you'll certainly hear the surf. The noise will be deafening. Don't panic. There's a cooler upstairs; bring it down here and fill it with ice. Oh, and you might want to cook that chicken." He shook her hand. "Good luck. *Courage!* You'll be fine."

Luli's hand trembled when she shook his, but she put on a brave face. "I can't thank you enough. Don't worry about me. I'm an old Girl Scout, y'know."

"Well, old girl, you're about to earn your hurricane badge!" he laughed. With a jaunty wave, he ran up the hill to his jeep. She heard him reverse out of the driveway and race away.

28

. . . .

LULI FELT SO ALONE AND SCARED SHE WANTED TO cry, but instead of withering, she got busy. She put the chicken to roast in the oven with butter, herbs, and balsamic vinegar, adding a few potatoes and carrots. Then she went back to cleaning the shelter, scrubbing the bathroom, the toilet, and shower stall until most of the moldy odor was gone. At least the place smelled better, even if it would never be spotless. She brought down soap, paper towels, toilet paper, a knife, a cutting board, pillows, a folding chair, her watercolors, sheets and towels, paper cups and plates, silverware, her books—there was no end to the list of what she might need for several days. She repacked her suitcase and dragged it down the hill. She filled every container she could find—pots and pans, plastic wastebaskets and tubs, pitchers, vases—with water and stored them in corners and the miniscule shower stall. When she finished washing out and drying the cooler, she added ice, then the food that needed refrigeration—fruit, cold cuts, vegetables, milk, cheese—and the chicken as soon as it was cool enough. Rummaging through the grocery bags, she found Jean-Luc had included several chocolate bars, a bottle of rum, limes, cans of Coke, and a pack of playing cards. "How did he know I'm a solitaire nut?" she wondered. "And the chocolate—good thinking."

Having put away and battened down everything she could think of, Luli sat on the porch watching the squall build. Dusk was an eerie matte red bleeding through dark clouds that descended over the bay, obscuring the setting sun. Night fell swiftly, all at once, like a heavy blanket. Angry clouds whisked the stars out of sight. Even the lights across the water disappeared as the gathering storm threatened to envelop everything in its opacity. The wind picked up, finally forcing her inside. She lay on the sofa, listening as the shutters rattled, and the gale whipped the trees into a frenzy. The electricity faltered, then went off completely. Guided by her flashlight beam, she left the house, closing the kitchen door firmly behind her. Powerful blasts of wind bent her almost double as she skidded down the incline to her cave.

Safe inside, she dragged the heavy metal door shut. It had two brackets welded onto each side of it. What are these for? She wondered. Then she noticed an iron bar leaning in a corner alongside the spars and reach poles. It was long enough to barricade the door. She dropped it into the hooks, lit the hurricane lamp, and built herself a nest of pillows on the mattress. Now what? Although a current of fresh air poured through the hole in the door, the room was stuffy and hot. She tried to read her Lisa Scottoline mystery, but after a page or two she began to doze. Preparing for the storm had exhausted her.

Over the clamor of the wind and pelting rain, she woke to someone pounding on the door.

"Luli! It's Jean-Luc. Open up! Better hang onto the door as best you can or we'll lose it," he yelled. "It's blowing like a son of a bitch out here."

Working together, the two managed to keep the door from flying off its hinges. Jean-Luc, dripping wet, slipped inside. He dropped a canvas duffle on the floor, and watched as Luli laid the iron bar across the door.

"Merde, alors," he said. "I hadn't noticed that set-up. Whoever built this dump must have experienced hurricanes." He stood shaking the rain off like a Labrador retriever, drying his hair with the towel Luli offered him. "Thanks. You can't imagine what a mess it already is out there. I thought the Jeep and I were going to be blasted into the bay. Believe me, I've been in bad storms, even a cyclone once in the South China Sea. But I've never seen a gale like this.

"I hope you won't mind my company. By the time we got the boats squared away inland, the markets were closed, the town was completely boarded up, and nobody was around. I told some friends I'd be here. This was the only place I could think of with good provisions."

"Like chocolate, rum, and roast chicken?" Luli said. "Vive la France!"

"Yeah," he smiled. "Exactly." He reached into the top of his bag, fumbled around, and brought forth a bottle of wine and a red-checkered tablecloth. "We frogs know how to live."

"Corkscrew?" Luli asked.

"Oh, shit. How could I have forgotten that?"

Luli pulled a Swiss Army knife out of her jeans pocket, pried out the corkscrew, and handed it to him. "Voilá. I told you I was a Girl Scout."

By the light of the hurricane lamp, Jean-Luc spread the tablecloth atop the cooler and they sat side by side on the mattress for a picnic supper of cold roast chicken, bread, and vegetables. "Oh, my. This is delicious," Jean Luc said. "Hope I'm not making a pig of myself. I'm ravenous."

"Maybe that's why it tastes so good."

He put down a chicken leg. "Madame, it tastes good because it IS good. You know how to cook." Luli grinned shyly. Jean-Luc poured wine into two paper cups and handed her one.

She took a sip. "Wow. This is the best wine I've ever tasted. What is it?"

"It's a Château Margaux, 1978. I've been saving it for a special occasion. I guess this will do. Santé!" he said, tapping his paper cup against hers.

The noise outside became deafening. Upstairs, shutters slammed against the windows, branches crashed to the ground. The rain assailed the cement walls of their shelter.

It was hard to talk above the shrieking of the wind. After dinner, they sat on the mattress leaning on pillows against the wall. "Are you sure the surge can't reach us?" she practically yelled into his ear. "It sounds awfully close." Water spurted in through the spy hole in powerful bursts, thwacking the door as if blasted from a power hose. The handkerchief Jean-Luc wadded into it was quickly soaked.

"I'd rather drown out there than in here," Luli said, clutching her arms to herself.

"Sissy! We're far enough up the cliff that the surf will never even come close. Jesus Christ," he scowled, "I hope you're not one of those whiners like some of my charter clients."

"And I hope you're not one of those snarly macho bastards who treat all women like brainless bimbos!" Luli retorted.

Jean-Luc wrung out his sodden, once white handkerchief and waved it with a conciliatory smile. "Truce?"

"OK, truce."

"I apologize. I know the surf sounds close, but it's the rain we're hearing, not waves," Jean-Luc reassured her.

"Damn, I'm exhausted. What a day! I'm going to try to get some sleep."

"I'm pretty tired myself," Luli said.

They lay down on the mattress at a discreet distance from one another and dozed. After a sleepless hour, Luli noticed Jean-Luc was awake.

"It's too noisy to sleep," she said.

"D'accord," Jean-Luc muttered.

Overhead, glass shattered on the terracotta floors. "I thought I had put away all the breakables, but I guess not," Luli said.

"Jesus, it sounds like a helluva barroom brawl up there."

"Hell's Angels partying on drugs," Luli said.

"Crystal meth, angel dust, blow, ecstasy, absinthe, firewater, the works."

Their laughter had an edge to it, but it helped cut the tension.

The storm banged on the house from all sides like a band of Paul Bunyan-sized drunken louts, smashing everything inside and out.

"By now, in case you're interested, the shutters, windows and doors have either blown into the house or they're half-way to France. Chairs, tables, all the furniture, everything's flying around," Jean-Luc said. "This sucker's strong enough to topple a refrigerator. I doubt the frame walls can withstand it. There won't be much left of the house, hélas. Jesus, I hope everyone's safe. This storm's a killer."

They heard a succession of loud cracks and booms. Their shelter shuddered. "There go the palm trees," Jean-Luc said. "I think at least one fell on the porch. Maybe on the house as well."

Luli was terrified. Would their sanctuary really hold? Its ceiling as well as its walls? Was he right about their being far enough away from the shore? Jean-Luc was confident, even excited. She had to trust him. And she had to put up a good front. She sat back on the mattress, resting on a pillow against the corner and observed him. A bit of the boy showed through his adult exterior whenever he pulled the handkerchief from his spy hole, held a piece of screen over it, and looked out. "Cool! This is fucking amazing," he reported. "Everything's flying sideways—branches, pieces of roofing. Jesus! There goes a satellite dish, spinning like a Frisbee. And an orange tree—roots and all. Wow! Come take a look at this!"

"Thanks. I think I'm good right where I am."

Jean Luc turned around and caught her watching him. He grinned like a kid discovered with his hand in a cookie jar. "You're sure you don't you want to take a look?"

"No thanks. I'm already scared shitless." She laughed and shook her head, strands of her sweat-soaked hair sticking to the sides of her face.

"What's so funny?"

"You remind me of my sons."

"How so?"

"As kids, my twin boys spent endless hours blowing up toy cars with firecrackers, shooting off bottle rockets, smashing caps on the sidewalks, throwing rocks at anything and everything. I drew the line at breaking glass bottles."

"Awwwww. What a party pooper!"

"Yes. And I made them clean up their messes."

"Luli, what does your sons' penchant for explosives have to do with a hurricane?"

"First, I have to ask you a question. What is it about the male person that positively delights in destruction and noise, especially violent dissonance like this storm?"

"It's fun! Exciting!" He thought for a moment, then shrugged. "Eh bien, shrinks probably have all sorts of theories about how it has to do with sex."

Luli laughed. "Everything has to do with sex. OK, I'll take a quick look." She crawled from her nest to his side, pulled out the kerchief, and held the patch of screen over the hole. Although it was dark outside, she could see the air was filled with all manner of flying debris, objects small and large spinning, whirring, crashing into each other.

"Yikes!" she said, shuddering, and returned the screen.

"Don't you think it's even a teenie bit cool?"

"No! It's awful! How will the island ever recover from this?"

He shrugged. "Life will go on. It always does, even after the worst of disasters."

Through the night, the wind railed at them, roaring like a chorus of lions, hissing, spitting, wailing. It hurled dirt against the shelter walls. Its force stole Luli's breath away and plugged up her ears. A cool draft blew in through the loosely blocked up spy hole, but it was hot and humid in the small room. The stale air made her groggy, but the racket kept her from sleeping. Her head throbbed. The wind's moods shifted, changing speed and direction, but never letting up.

Jean-Luc looked out again and laughed. "Christ. Now it's blowing sideways the other way. I've never seen anything like this. Here's your chance to get a good view of a genuine hurricane. You're absolutely sure you don't want another peek?"

"Uh huh," Luli said.

While Luli tried to nap, Jean-Luc busied himself fiddling with the radio. Reception was terrible. Signals, crackling and rent by static, faded in and out. He found an English-speaking station from Nevis that reported on the storm's path of destruction as it slammed from island to island.

Repeatedly, the announcer told listeners to remain in their shelters. "When the wind seems to be diminishing, it is the eye of the storm passing through. Do not go outside," the announcer said emphatically in his lilting Caribbean English. "There will be more violent winds for some time. We will give you the all clear when the hurricane has blown over. Please stay tuned and stay safe."

Jean-Luc upended his sea bag onto the shelter's cement floor. Clothes, a dopp kit, books, shoes, and assorted things spilled out. "Aha!" he said, rummaging through the duffle's contents to produce a boxed Scrabble game. "You wouldn't by chance be a Scrabble player, would you?"

"Oh, my God. I haven't played in years. You're probably an ace."

"No, I'm a rank amateur."

"Emphasis on 'rank.' Phew—I wish you'd showered before you foisted yourself on me."

"Je le regret, madame. I will attempt to repair my odiferous honor by stomping you. My kind of Scrabble is where you score fifty extra points for a good cuss word. Once in a while I play a game with my charter clients. It can be boring out at sea. So, madame, might I interest you in a friendly game?"

"OK, but no French. And nix on the cuss words. You're a sailor. You have an unfair advantage."

"Arrrrrggghhh," Jean-Luc said.

"And no pirate slang, either. You'll still beat me by thousands of points. I'm as rusty as . . . as the hinges on that door."

"Damn, I sure hope they hold."

Jean-Luc played well, but to her surprise, Luli was better than she thought she would be. He liked to double up on words, getting extra points by making a word that read in two or more directions. He was very proud of himself when he played two letters forming words four ways.

Luli pointed to the "et" he put down. "Excuse me—I thought we agreed, no French," she protested. "That's French. And it's also Latin. No fair!"

Jean-Luc pouted. "It's the chemical symbol for ethyl."

"No symbols or abbreviations. It's in the rules."

"It's the little green guy who phones home."

"No proper nouns."

He thought for a second. "'Et' is also English! Colloquial British English. Past participle of 'eat'. As in 'we haven't yet et dessert.'"

"You're pulling my leg. Well, I'll let it go, just this once. Come to think of it, though, we haven't yet *et* dessert, have we?"

They cut wedges of Roquefort, sliced pears, and sipped wine while they continued to play.

Jean-Luc won by a hearty hundred points. "Revanche, madame?"

"If that means revenge, I'm all for it."

They gathered up the tiles, and picked letters out of a bag for another round. This time Luli came within twenty points of winning.

"I think we'd better quit while I'm ahead," Jean-Luc said.

"Chicken!" Luli said. "Truth is, I'm not really tired, but I feel stupid. Why is that?"

"It is obvious, madame. I am so much smarter."

Luli scoffed.

"Actually it's the wind. It sucks all the oxygen out of the air. I don't feel like the sharpest pencil in the box myself."

They lay down on the mattress. Although they were bone tired, neither slept. After a while, Jean-Luc turned on his side to face her. He could see she was still awake. "I will tell you what happened with Flip," he said.

"Whatever it is, I know it's extremely painful. You're not obliged to tell me a thing."

"I know. But I want to. The only person I ever talked to about Flip was my wife, Sarah. She's gone now."

Opening her eyes, Luli saw his were filling with tears.

"Gone as in she died from cancer, breast cancer. Five years ago."

"Oooh, how heart breaking. For you and your family. I'm so sorry," she said softly.

He took a deep breath. "We've easily got another twenty-four hours in these palatial surroundings. It will pass the time—my sad tale of woe," he said with a bitter laugh.

"When I was seven and Henri, my brother, was five, our mother—Sylvie—took off for Switzerland, where she was born, with the tennis pro from our country club on Long Island. We never saw her again. She'd send us birthday cards and, at Christmas, boxes of fancy French clothes we refused to wear. They were always the wrong sizes anyway. When I was ten, she and her new husband—not the tennis pro—were killed in a car crash in the Alps. I gather she was driving. Chances are, she was plastered. Eugènie, the aunt who became my real mother, told me she was as much a drinker as my dad. I hardly remember her.

"Father did the best he could, I guess. But he was an alcoholic, so his best was pretty piss-poor. After Mother split, we moved to an apartment in the same building in Manhattan as Eugènie and Uncle Randolph, Flip's brother. Voilà, we were not only an extended family, we were a dysfunctional extended family. Randolph was as bad a lush as Flip. The brothers would go on benders together. They were stockbrokers on Wall Street, in the firm my grandfather founded. Flip was rarely home when we were awake. My aunt and our maid, Zenda, would have us in bed by the time he came in, way late, reeking of booze. He'd stagger into our bedroom to wish us a good night. I could smell him before I saw him. I turned away pretending to be asleep to avoid his noxious kiss. In the morning, he'd be gone. He also worked weekends, or he and my uncle would disappear into the University Club bar to play cards and get soused. It was really Eugènie who raised us. She went to our soccer matches, our dental appointments, our parent-teacher conferences. She was a kind, loving, generous person. Whatever shreds of decency I have in me, are her doing."

"Is she still alive?"

"Oh, yes, very much so. She's in her late seventies. Still lives in her Manhattan apartment. My daughters—I've got three—adore her. Randolph died years ago."

"Three daughters. That's terrific. I've got two, and two boys—the destructo twins."

"You know, every man thinks he wants sons, not daughters. But I'll tell you, my girls mean everything to me. They're the best. Boys grow up and move away. Daughters, even if they don't live close by, dote on you. Emilie, the oldest one, was supposed to come to visit next week with her husband and toddlers. Now they'll have to cancel."

"You're a grandfather?"

"Mais, oui. The salty old dog is a grandpère. I have to watch my language around the kids. A boy and a girl. How I treasure them! They love visiting here, the fourth generation to call Ste. Foi home. I take them sailing every chance I get."

Even in the dimness, Luli could see Jean-Luc's eyes light up. Then he became somber again.

"The only time we saw much of Father was on vacations when we'd come to our house here—Christmas, Easter, and for the summer. Eugènie was always with us. Uncle Randolph and Flip would come for the month of August. We all stayed in the Maison Azure, just down the beach from here.

"That picturesque blue house with the wrap-around porch?"

"Yes. Their father built it in the twenties. When they were small, Flip and Randolph spent their vacations here. We adored Ste. Foi, and so did our aunt. We made a pact to speak nothing but French on the island. She's a Parisienne who met Randolph here.

"For Henri and me, this place was heaven, especially when the drunks weren't around. We went barefoot all summer. We were only required to wear shoes to Mass on Sundays because my aunt insisted. We spent our days sailing, snorkeling, spear fishing, rowing. We rode bikes everywhere. We hung out with the local kids. Everybody on the island knew us and looked out for us. Madame DuFour even gave us free croissants."

"Sounds fabulous."

"It was. New York was fun at times, but the school we went to was very strict. Even in our largish apartment, I always felt like I was on a short leash. I lived for the time we spent on Ste. Foi.

"Then, when I was almost thirteen and Henri was eleven—it was in August and Father was here—there was a terrible accident."

Jean-Luc hesitated and stared off into space. "Henri and I were messing around late one afternoon in a leaky wooden dinghy about fifty feet off shore. We were having a war, standing in the boat batting at each other with oars—the kind of stupid stuff boys do. Flip was on the porch watching us, sucking on a tall one. He yelled at us a couple of times to stop, but we ignored him. When Henri gave me a pretty good whack in the shoulder, I hit him back even harder. We both lost our balance. The dinghy was never very stable anyway. It tipped over."

Jean-Luc paused for a moment, examining his hands.

"I understand if you want to stop right there, Jean-Luc."

He shook his head and continued.

"I was under the upside down boat. It was sinking on top of me. I tried to come up, but it was pushing me down. When I realized what was happening, I tried swimming to the side, to swim out from under it. Just as I was about to give up, I saw it—the fabled golden light. I quit struggling and reached for it. I felt peaceful and calm. I was no longer fighting for air. I wasn't in any pain. I stroked toward the light. Then, to my immense surprise, I broke through the surface. I took a huge gulp of air and looked around for Henri, but he hadn't come up. I screamed for Dad. 'Henri's drowning! Henri's drowning, Father! Help us, somebody! Please help!' But Father wasn't on the porch. He'd probably gone inside to pour another drink.

"I dove I don't know how many times, but I couldn't find Henri in the fading light. It was about thirty feet deep there, and almost dark on a moonless night. Finally, I saw a foot sticking out from under the boat's gunwales where it had settled on the ocean floor. I tried to lift it off him, but I couldn't. I surfaced, screaming again for help. This time, Maribelle's husband, Antoine, came running. He swam out to me. We both tried to budge the boat but it was useless. Other men came. By the time there were enough of them to lift the dinghy and pull Henri out from under it, fifteen minutes had passed. We couldn't get him breathing again. He was dead."

In the light from the lantern, Luli could see Jean-Luc's face was bathed in tears. She laid her hand on his shoulder.

"Flip came out onto the porch to see what the ruckus was. I distinctly remember he had a full glass in his hand. I screamed at him. 'You fucker! You miserable, useless fucking drunk!'

"When he saw the men carrying my brother onto the beach, he dropped the glass and clumsily scrambled over the porch railing. He fell and rolled down the hill to the beach. But he was too late, way too late.

"I can't tell you how many million times since then I see myself on the bottom of the bay, trying my damnedest to lift that goddamn boat, trying to pull my brother out from under it. Or I try to erase the memory where Henri and I are going at each other with the oars before the boat flipped. I dream we put down our oars and quit fighting. Sarah said I often woke up screaming at night, but I don't remember. All I know is that it was by far the worst experience of my life. I'll never get over it. Never. I killed my brother."

Tears streamed down Jean-Luc's face, and his jaw was clenched in pain. In the dim light Luli handed him a roll of toilet paper. "Jean-Luc, you didn't kill your brother. Don't do that to yourself. It was an accident, an awful one. You did the best you could to save him. It could as easily have been you under that sinking boat rather than Henri."

He wiped his face roughly with the crumpled tissue, and abruptly rolled over with his back to her. She curled around him, holding him as if he were one of her children. Neither spoke. Eventually, they both slept.

When she awoke, Jean-Luc was up, refilling the lamp with kerosene by the light from several fat candles set in saucers. Outside, the wind continued to whistle, wheeze, and whack on the door. Above, boards from the porch flooring or the side of the house flapped madly in the gale, making a terrible din.

Luli groaned. "Is it morning?"

"Well, my watch says it's 7:30 a.m."

"What does the peephole have to say?"

"It's still pretty dark out there. The wind's blowing hard as ever. The radio says we'll have at least another twenty-four hours of this."

"Ugh. Jeez, my head hurts. It can't be a hangover. There's still half a bottle of wine, and it was the best I've ever had. Maybe it's caffeine deprivation."

"More likely oxygen depletion. But, madame, you're in luck. There's café in my thermos. It's a day old, and not exactly piping hot, but it has the requisite caffeine. For today's petit-déjeuner, madame's private chef—moi—offers stale French bread, butter, jam. Oh, there's also some sliced ham, if you like."

"Fantastique! J'ai faim!"

29

. . . .

THE DAY PASSED SLOWLY. THEY PLAYED SCRABBLE and slumbered between games. Around two in the afternoon, the wind diminished somewhat, although it was still blowing hard.

"Maybe the eye's passing over us," Jean-Luc said.

"Good news, I suppose. Although that would mean we're only half way through this, right?"

Jean-Luc fiddled with the radio. Catching a station from Guadeloupe, he put his ear against the speaker. Especially with the static interference, the French was so fast and garbled Luli couldn't understand it.

He translated for her. "Yes, we're in the eye, it seems. Pretty soon, the other side of the hurricane will blast through here. God, I hope everyone made it to port in time. This thing would toss ocean liners around like tub toys."

"I can't thank you enough for coming to my rescue," Luli said. "I would have been terrified in here all by myself. You saved my life. I had no idea we were in for something like this. Not a clue. I wondered why people were rushing around town yesterday. I thought maybe there was going to be a big party."

"Some party. How about a game of cards?"

"Sure. But I never remember the rules to card games, so you'll have to tell me."

"You trust me?"

"Of course not."

They played hearts, and Luli won. "This calls for a glass of wine," she said. "I'm sure the sun is past the yardarm, sailor."

"If the captain says it is, it is. You're the captain of this royal barge, you know." He poured the remaining wine into their soggy paper cups. They played another game of hearts.

Soon Jean-Luc lay down and began to talk, almost to himself. His arms crossed behind his head, he stared at the ceiling. "So there I was, a twelve-year-old kid with a drunk for a father, a long-gone mother. All of a sudden, I was also brotherless. I felt very sorry for myself. Flip drank worse than ever, school was a drag. The only person I could talk to was Eugènie. And Zenda. My dear, precious, magnificent Jamaican mama, the person who tended me from my birth, who raised me as if I were her own, who never failed me— unlike my parents. She probably never had children of her own because she had Henri and me to look after. As well as Flip, her third kid.

"Then one afternoon when I came home from school— I'd just turned fifteen—Eugènie sat me down and told me Flip was 'disparu.' I wasn't sure whether she was politely saying he was dead or that he had disappeared. The word can mean either. 'What are you telling me?' I asked her.

"'He's not dead, but he said he had to leave. Every time he looks at you he sees your dead brother. Jean-Luc, he can't bear it. Your mother left because of his drinking, he couldn't save Henri because he was drunk, he doesn't think he's doing you any good . . .'

"'He's deserting me?' I was outraged. '*He* can't bear it? What about *me*? How does he think this situation is for *me*? No mother, no brother, and now, no father?'

"'He knows perfectly well how he has failed you. He loves you, he truly does. But he thinks he's a rotten parent . . .'"

"'He's got that right,' I said.

"Flip made Eugènie and Randolph my legal guardians. He put his assets into a trust for me. My aunt gave me the note he left. The paper was so tear-stained the writing was almost illegible. The letter was full of apologies. Over and over, he said he loved me, that he was doing the best thing for me. Given the penchant for drama common to teenagers, I put a match to the paper and tossed it into the fireplace. Soggy or not, it went right up in flames.

"He wanted me to go to his prep school, Andover, because he went there. I lasted a couple of years. I was surely the angriest kid in the school. In no time, I was into drugs. I was a troublemaker—sarcastic, surly, violent, a thoroughly rotten kid. The school did what they could for me, but finally, they kicked me out for good.

"I'd had enough anyway. I joined the Merchant Marine. It was the smartest move I ever made—except for marrying Sarah. I learned marine engines, seamanship, self-discipline, and I saw a lot of the world."

"Tell me about the tiger tattoo on your ankle."

"Ah, you noticed."

"I'm a mom. I've reared four teenagers. I notice these things."

"Singapore. Shore leave. I got stinking drunk. When I woke up a day later back on the ship, my head feeling like it was in a vise, there it was. Quelle surprise!

"By twenty-two, I was ready to go back to school. And I did. Miraculously, Yale took me in once I passed admissions tests. I never actually graduated from high school."

"You and Albert Einstein. Yale, huh. That's impressive."

"I'm sure Flip had paved the way for me with a generous gift. Or maybe an appeal to a classmate of his who had been provost of the university. I studied engineering, then went to work for a firm in Manhattan that built bridges all over the world. But I got myself in trouble with drugs again. Big trouble this time—cocaine, mostly. I snorted my way through a wad of money. The company fired me. I came down here to kick around. There were more drugs here than even in Manhattan. I went apeshit.

"Jesus, am I boring you?"

"Hell, no. I mean, considering what a rotten childhood you had, I'm not surprised in the least you turned to drugs for relief."

"But they made everything much worse."

"Of course."

"This is where the cobs come in. I knew Flip kept them in a safe on the island. Because he left Manhattan in kind of a hurry, I didn't think he took them with him when he bailed. I knew his coins meant a lot to him, probably more than I did . . ."

"I doubt that. But you had every right in the world to be furious with him and want revenge."

"Maybe. Well, not maybe. I did want revenge. With the help of a semi-retired thief who lived on the island, I got into the safe in the unused cistern under the Maison. I started living off the coins like they were spare change. I traded them for drugs, probably for a hundredth of what they were worth."

"Somebody told Eugènie I was paying my way down here with gold coins. She got on the next flight and put a stop to it. She took what was left of the collection with her to New York, and insisted I go into rehab in the States. She said if I didn't, she'd cut me out of her life. Zenda called me from Jamaica, where she'd retired. She gave me the same ultimatum. I couldn't bear to lose the only two people in the world who truly loved me.

"It took several tries, a lot of therapy. I was in and out of institutions for two years before I could kick the stuff. I talked my former firm into taking me back on probation. Bless them, they did. Then I met Sarah. She convinced me that life without drugs was worth living.

"Your turn."

"What a wretched life you had, Luc, at least, until you got sober. Please go on."

"No, your turn. I want to hear about your life, Luli. I've talked too much."

She hesitated. "Well, my story's nowhere near as dramatic—or awful—as yours. I grew up in a small town along the Fox River south of Green Bay in northeastern Wisconsin. My dad drank a lot, my mother suffered in silence—or in screaming fits—and shoved everything under the living room rug. The priests told her Dad was her cross to bear and heaven would be her reward. I went to college in Madison. I wanted to major in art—I always wanted to be a painter—but my parents insisted on something more practical, so I got a degree in education. I married my college sweetheart, we were blessed with four fabulous kids, the real loves of my life, and I rarely got to paint anything more than their bedrooms. Six months ago, my alcoholic husband cleaned out our bank accounts, mortgaged our home in an attempt to cover his business debts, sold all our assets, took the money, and ran. Accompanied by our former babysitter, a trollop half his age. Now I'm a dumped ex-wife cleaning houses for a living in Santa Fe."

"Christ, what a stupid asshole he must be."

"Uh huh."

"Surely there's more. This sounds like the Cliff Notes for your life story."

"Of course there's more, but it's not that interesting."

"I'll bet it is. Try me."

"Only if you break out the chocolate."

Nibbling a Toblerone bar, Luli told about finding Flip bleeding in the Kaune's parking lot and meeting the Alires.

"Wait. Back up. Didn't you tell me your father was an alcoholic?"

"Yes. Some of the time he behaved and he'd have a couple of Manhattans in the evening. But nearly every month, he'd go on a binge for two or three days. It was my older brother's duty to go find him in one of his regular bars and bring him home. That was my brother Nat; he was killed in Vietnam."

"Oh, my. How dreadful."

She nodded. "He was eight years older than me, my best buddy. The week before he was due to come home, he stepped on a land mine. Poof! I still miss him. I think about him all the time."

"I miss Henri. Constantly. It's like he's away on a trip. One that has gone on far too long. I sure wish he'd come home. Go on."

"One night when I was twelve or so, Dad came home drunk as a … sailor. I was kind of a priss then, self-righteous, definitely in the grip of the nuns. I yelled at him. 'I used to think you were a smart man. But you're just an alkie, no better than the bums that hang out around the blood center in Green Bay!'"

"What did he do?"

"He came after me like a rabid Rottweiler. I ran upstairs to my room. He was right behind me. I couldn't close the door fast enough. I knew from his yelling he was going to beat the living shit out of me. . . ." She stopped, chewing on her nails, her heart throbbing like a bad wound.

"I fell back on the bed. When he pounced on me, I kicked him in the stomach, sent him flying across the room. He hit his head on my dresser and was knocked out, his head all bloody. I was scared silly. I thought I'd killed him."

"Goddamn, that must have been terrifying. At least Flip never hit us."

"The next day, Dad said he was overworked, he'd drunk way too much, and he never meant to harm me."

"Did he quit drinking?"

"Of course not. He still had his daily measure and went on benders. When Nat left for Vietnam, the task of fetching him home from the bars fell to my younger brother, Bart. But Dad never came after me again.

"My freshman year, when I came home from college at Christmas, an old high school friend asked me, 'Is it true your Dad kicked Judge Thompson in the balls at the Kaukauna Keglers Bar and got thrown in jail?'

"I was horrified. Judge Thompson! He was a local hero who'd lost a leg in Italy during WW II. I asked my mother what happened. 'I've never heard of such a thing,' she sniffed and walked off. This was her way of dealing with Dad's drinking—to make like none of it ever happened. Finally, his liver gave out. He died a few months after I graduated from college."

"What a heartbreaker."

"It was, but in a way, it was a relief. He was awful to take care of. The cops would arrest him for DWI. He hid bottles in the toilet tanks, in the trunk of his car—the usual drunkard's tricks. Once he even emptied out a container of Murphy's Oil Soap and filled it with cheap whiskey instead. When Mother went to mop the kitchen floor, she discovered the ruse. She was furious, and threw one of her screaming fits. After he died, my mother went to work at a local dress shop. She was thrilled to be out of the house, the customers loved her, so did the owners. At 82, she still works there.

"You know, all this yakking has made me famished. If you want, I can make us chicken salad for supper."

"Bonne idée, madame."

While she cut up chicken, tomatoes, leftover potatoes, added lettuce, and dressed the salad with a vinaigrette, Jean-Luc asked her more about her childhood.

"Stop me if I'm getting overly personal," he said.

"I don't mind it's not like we're rushing off anywhere, you know. When you talk about your vacations here on Ste. Foi, it reminds me of our summers in Door County. In the 1800s, my mother's Norwegian grandfather built a beautiful big beachstone cottage on the shore in a lovely village called Fish Creek. Poppa Pettersen was famous for his stonework and carpentry. Wealthy people from Chicago and Milwaukee had him build their summer palaces for them along the shore on a road that came to be called Millionaires' Row. But he did his best work on the home he built for his own family. In fact, the money we're getting from renting it out is helping keep my kids in college.

"Your husband didn't borrow on that house as well?"

"No. Fortunately, I owned it before I married so in the divorce it wasn't community property."

"Brava!"

"Oh, yeah. I heard Herb was really pissed off when he discovered he couldn't get at the place. Arguing about it with the judge made things worse for him."

"Where exactly is Door County? I don't know that part of the country."

"It's in Wisconsin, the peninsula separating Green Bay from Lake Michigan to the east. It's very beautiful— about a hundred miles long, limestone cliffs, little Moravian villages, birch trees on the bay side. On the lake side, there are lovely white sand beaches, dunes, thimbleberry bushes, marshes, parks. Quite another ecology. A canal cuts through the Peninsula at the southern edge in Sturgeon Bay, technically making Door County an island.

"We never wore shoes in summer either—except to go to Mass. We went sailing, swimming, fishing, waterskiing. We poached golf games on the private course after they closed for the evening. For pocket money, we hunted for golf balls, picked cherries when they were in season, and babysat for the families on Millionaire's Row. As long as we were home for supper at six, nobody knew or cared where we were. In many ways, it was idyllic.

"Salad's done," she announced. "I'm so hungry. How can I have such an appetite? All we've done is loll around, eat, drink, and talk."

"I think it's those vicious Scrabble games. Real calorie-burners."

They finished the chicken salad in short order. Outside, the wind swirled no less lustily, but everything that could have been wrenched off its mooring was long gone—or so it seemed. A few loose boards upstairs still whapped against the house.

Jean-Luc bent his ear to the radio and gave her the latest news. "The tail end of the hurricane passed Martinique a little while ago. The front end has almost reached Puerto Rico. This storm is huge. We're still in the thick of it. Maybe by tomorrow it will have blown over us."

"Is that what the radio says—or is it your wishful thinking?"

"Both. Say—are you up for another round of Scrabble?"

Late that night, as they lay on the mattress trying to sleep, Jean-Luc said, "I've been thinking about the cobs. If Flip wants them, I'm sure Eugènie would ship him what's left of his collection. With the price of gold as high as it is, plus their collecting value, he'd be able to sell them for a lot of money."

"What about your girls?"

"They're well taken care of, especially because Sarah came from a wealthy family. My marina actually turns a profit, although the hurricane's going to rip holes in my income for a while. Much as I tried in my druggie days to blow through the assets in my trust, I didn't succeed. Eugènie's in excellent financial shape. So is Zenda. When Father left New York, he gave her a pension and enough to buy herself a house in Jamaica.

"The cobs are Father's," he added. "I don't care what he does with them."

"He wants to leave money to organizations that help people like him, people who've been victimized by a family member's alcoholism or drug addictions, especially battered women and children. Like he said in the documents I gave you. Did you read them?"

"Yes. And I'm all for it," Jean-Luc said. He turned his back to her and fell asleep.

30

. . . .

By morning, the winds had died down. Jean-Luc peered out the peephole. "It's not blowing very hard. Do you think we should open the door?"

"But what if it's not over? What if it's only a lull? Then where would we be?"

"Probably Cabo Verde?"

Just then, they heard the thwack of an axe and voices. "Jean-Luc? Où te trouves?" a man shouted.

"Ici!" he yelled back. "Nous sommes ici, en bas. Dans la citerne!"

He took the bar off the door and leaned against it, trying to push it open; it wouldn't budge. Luli shoved with him, but they could only move it a couple of inches, enough to see that it was blocked by downed trees, and trash.

"We can't open the door!" Jean-Luc shouted in French.

They heard four men crashing through the vegetation, beating their way toward them with axes and machetes.

Suddenly Luli felt claustrophobic and faint. "If we don't bust out of this hole pretty soon, I think I'm going to seriously freak," she said in a quavering voice. "I'm not joking. I'm seeing sparks."

"Stick with me," Jean-Luc said, continuing to push outward. "No fading violets at this point in the game. *Courage!* Get in touch with your inner Girl Scout, Luli!"

The noise of bushwhacking outside told them Luc's friends had almost reached their shelter. Luli picked up a gaff and tried to insert it in the crack between the door and the frame.

"Bonne idée!" Jean-Luc said. He took over, using the pole as a pry bar, widening the opening bit by bit. A filtered light streamed in through the widened crack, enabling them to see that outside, downed debris was piled up almost the entire height of the cistern. They would never be able to escape without help.

Outside, the men worked furiously, hacking at felled branches, casting them aside, making a path to the shelter and clearing a space in front of the door.

Finally, attacking the blocked exit from both sides, pushing and pulling, they were able to open the door partway. As soon as the opening was wide enough, Jean-Luc shoved Luli through, then followed her out. They scrambled over huge mounds of trees and palm fronds like dazed insects, squinting from the half-light that seemed painfully bright after sixty hours in semi-darkness. The men seemed surprised to see a good-looking, if bedraggled woman with Luc, but made no comment.

An ugly perversion of a tropical travel poster greeted them.

"Oh, my God!" Luli gasped. Her eyes welled up as she gazed at the destruction. All along the hillside overlooking the bay, boarded up houses, some with their roofs gone, some blown off their foundations, stood naked and topsy-turvy along the cliff, surrounded by heaps of smashed greenery. Not a single leaf was left on the few trees and bushes that had withstood the winds. A war had devastated the landscape. A nuclear bomb had exploded, leveling all in its path. Everything was colorless, lifeless, the sky a low-hanging, washed out dirty gray flannel, the sea still dark and churning, hurling massive waves at a beach already scraped bare to its coral reef bones. Inland, every surface was coated with a sodden mess of mashed vegetation that made Luli think of pesto, but smelled like rotting garbage.

Jean-Luc had been right about the pink house being too fragile to withstand such a violent storm. All but two of the palm trees that surrounded it had fallen through part of the tin roof that was peeled back on itself like the lid on a sardine can. What was left of the cottage was open to the pewter sky. With only two partial walls left standing, the house was a total loss, destroyed as effectively as if a wrecking ball had struck it repeatedly. Shutters and screens hung limply from empty window frames. Cracked pink boards lay like matchsticks on the tile floor, and more were scattered around the yard. The storm had broken every-thing that could break. Luli trembled at the thought of what would have happened to her if Jean-Luc hadn't come along.

He shook hands with each of the four men. "How are things on the island?" he asked with trepidation.

"Tout cassé," one said shaking his head sadly. "Everything on the coast is busted, but it's better inland. Your boats are probably safe. We're going house to house to check on everyone. So far, a few broken bones, some bad cuts, but no deaths, grâce à Dieu. When we saw your Jeep, we came looking for you, hoping you weren't in that house."

"Merci, copains. We couldn't have gotten out of the citerne without you. We'll help check on other people. Is my Jeep in one piece?"

"It's tipped on its side and has a cracked windshield, but no trees fell on it. We'll right it and clear the driveway so you can drive out."

"Luli, let's round up bottles of water, food, find some tools, and get going. That is, if you feel up to it. I'm sure others are buried like we were."

"I'm fine. Let's go."

They drove down the road, stopping to drag tree limbs and other obstructions off the pavement. At every dwelling, people crawled out from under their wrecked houses, bedraggled and dazed. They wandered through the thickets of felled trees as if they'd been drugged, taking stock of their buildings, animals, cars, boats, and gardens. Luli watched as a man in an undershirt and shorts picked up a scrap of corrugated roofing, then a palm frond, and finally, a banged-up bucket. Befuddled, he cast about, trying to decide what to do with the misplaced objects. Where to begin?

In the driveway of a partially destroyed B & B, two young tourist couples, remarkably cheerful in their sweaty, grimy clothes, slipped on the puree of leaves that coated the asphalt as they gathered grinning for a group photo. Beside a house Jean-Luc said belonged to Madame DuFour's sister, a teenage boy hacked angrily with an axe at a huge tree crushing the bow of a once shiny speedboat on a trailer. Unlike the tourists, he wasn't amused. His mother kept shaking her head as she worked barefoot, slashing a machete through the wreckage surrounding her house.

"Is everyone safe?" Jean-Luc asked her.

"Yes, thank you. We're all unhurt. Mais je suis si fatiguée. Can you help me find my rabbits? A branch fell on their hutch. Maybe they died of fright."

For the next week, Luli worked with Jean-Luc, checking on islanders at their homes, driving those needing medical treatment to a makeshift clinic in the high school gym, rescuing cats, dogs, chickens and clearing brush. At night, they'd return to the shelter to collapse in exhaustion on the mattress. The days passed like calendar pages flipped by a breeze. With the locals and tourists, they queued up for groceries, bottled water, and gas, exchanging news of how they'd fared in l'ouragan, and wishing each other *courage*.

To everyone's relief, the storm hadn't killed anyone on Ste. Foi, although many islanders had lost everything. Dozens of people had died elsewhere in the Leewards, especially on the less prosperous islands where houses were not as well-built and sturdy shelters were rare. On Guadeloupe, a German photographer had been swept off a pier on the first night by a killer wave while he tried to take pictures of the tempest. More people were injured or killed in the looting and burning after the storm, adding to the islanders' misery. By contrast, the only looting Luli and Jean-Luc saw on Ste. Foi was a father and his two tow-headed sons gleefully scooping up armloads of felled coconuts from the parking lot of a fancy hotel and carting them off in a wheelbarrow.

French Air Force transport planes began to land on the island. They disgorged cadres of young conscripts who fixed power and telephone lines and helped islanders rebuild. Inexperienced gendarmes screwed up traffic, to the locals' amusement. A teenage girl Luli hadn't seen before came out of Madame DuFour's sister's house to work alongside the soldiers, or at least flirt with them.

Finally one evening as Luli and Jean-Luc lay down after supper, Luli said, "It's time for me to leave."

Jean-Luc said nothing. He buried his face in her shoulder and wrapped his arms around her.

At the airport, small private planes were still flipped on their backs like dead cockroaches. French military helicopters landed and took off in squadrons. Boxes containing chain saws, portable generators, and other supplies were stacked along the runway. Soldiers unloaded more cartons from a huge cargo plane.

As the stewardess of the airliner to Puerto Rico stood at the bottom of the ladder waiting for passengers to board, Jean-Luc and Luli held each other for a very long time. She started to say goodbye, but with a smile as luminous as the sunlight reflected off the ocean, he put his finger to her lips.

31

· · · · · · ·

BACK IN SANTA FE, LULI WAS LONELY AND AT LOOSE ends. The Alires, Sammy, and a few others were initially interested in hearing about her hurricane adventure. They looked gape-mouthed at the photos she took of Ste. Foi after the storm. But as vivid as the hurricane remained to Luli, it was last week's TV news to those who hadn't lived it. The people with whom she'd shared the intense, terrifying experience were still on the island, trying to put their lives and livelihoods back together. No one said *courage* to her in Santa Fe's grocery stores.

Luli's children chided her for not phoning them. "We saw pictures of the hurricane on television. We were so worried about you, Mom. Why didn't you call us sooner?"

"There were no landlines and cell phone towers were down. All I could do was pass on a message via a ham operator to say I was alive and well, which I did as soon as I possibly could."

"No phones?" Her kids, who were rarely without cell phones stuck to their ears, couldn't fathom it.

"No electricity, no running water, no mail, no way off the island. But people pulled together to help each other. It was an amazing experience."

While Luli was in Ste. Foi, Flip had suffered another relapse. When he was well enough to go home from St. Vincent's, she and the Alires picked him up. He looked more frail than ever. They put him to bed and tried to feed him, but he wouldn't eat. The next day, he nibbled at a modest breakfast and said he felt stronger. He was eager to talk to Luli. He was more interested than anyone in hearing about the hurricane. His eyes lit up when she mentioned Madame DuFour's mother.

"My God. That old toothpick's still alive? She must be at least a hundred and fifty. It's a wonder she didn't blow away."

"She's 93 now. Two days after the hurricane, she was back making two hundred pains ficelles a day. She said this ouragan was worse than the ones in 1950 and 1960."

"Those were terrible storms," Flip said, a sadness filling his eyes. "I remember visiting a few months after the 1960 one. The island was a shambles."

"May I ask for a report on your journey?"

"Of course. You paid for it, after all."

Luli related meeting Jean-Luc at the café. "I knew who he was the minute I saw him. He looks a lot like you." Skipping the part about his initial hostility, she told Flip about their sharing the cistern shelter and working together after the hurricane in the relief effort. "People on the island think the world of him. He's been through some decidedly difficult times, especially with drugs, but he's beyond that phase of his life. He grieves for his wife, but cherishes your granddaughters and great-grandchildren. Your son is a fine man. You should be very proud of him.

"Flip, why haven't you ever contacted Jean-Luc?"

He hung his head. "I can never forgive myself for Henri's death. Even before that, I was a disgusting wretch, useless as a father. After I deserted Luc, I couldn't face any of my family, especially not him. I'm no good to anyone—not even myself."

His eyes watered. For a long time, he blinked back tears. When he looked up at Luli again, however, his eyes were clear. "May I make a confession?" he asked in a soft voice.

"Sure."

"I've been in contact with Eugènie intermittently as the years passed, although not for a while. I've followed Jean-Luc's life, his downs and ups. I knew he lost his wife. I never met her, but everyone says she was fabulous, and they were very happy together. I know I've got granddaughters, and I'm not surprised to learn I also have great grandchildren."

He hesitated, then sheepishly looked at Luli. "I also knew Eugènie is in possession of the remainder of my cobs."

Luli exploded. "WHAT? You skunk, Flip! Excuse my French, but why the hell did you send me on that wild goose chase? I was in a hurricane. I could have been killed."

"I didn't know about the hurricane."

"But why, Flip? Goddammit, what was that trip all about?"

He tipped his head to the side, regarded Luli obliquely, and smiled mischievously.

Luli continued to clean houses. With a more or less reliable income, she signed up for an accounting class at the Santa Fe Community College. She found it exhausting to work long, hard days, then try to use her brain in the evenings for something more mentally challenging than following the directions on the oven cleaner can. But she loved the class.

"I really enjoy keeping people's books for them," she told the Alires. "It's very satisfying when the numbers square."

She often thought about Jean-Luc, but she was too shy to write him. What would she say? Two weeks after her return, she got a letter from him. It began: "Why haven't you written me? Are you all right? I miss you. I miss beating you at Scrabble."

She responded immediately. "Is that all I'm good for—losing to you? Revanche!"

They began to phone each other almost every night, although Jean-Luc insisted on paying for the calls. Luli was anxious to hear about the island's recovery. Most of the boats he and his men had taken inland were undamaged, including his own. The marina needed major repairs. The French government was continuing to ferry in supplies to help people rebuild. "Unlike in the States, the government is forcing insurance companies to pay up fast and generously," he told her. "It'll be a year at least before the tourism business gets back on its feet, though."

"How are people coping?"

"Ah, you know us French. We greet it all with a Gallic shrug," Jean-Luc laughed. "C'ést la vie. The rains are helping the vegetation recover. We might even get an expanded health clinic out of all this. Madame DuFour's niece and the other island girls are enjoying the French soldiers' company. It's not all negative. In fact, I've never seen this place so alive. It's an anthill. People are rebuilding like crazy, working all hours. Even former adversaries are helping each other out."

He hesitated. "I miss you dreadfully, Luli."

"I miss you, too," she said.

Luli lay on the couch one afternoon after work with her feet up, reading a newspaper when Adán rapped on her door.

"Come in!"

"It's Flip. He's off the wagon again. The ambulance took him this morning after you went to work. Dr. Pacheco says he might not make it this time. We're driving to the hospital now to visit him. Do you want to go?"

Flip's eyes were closed when Luli and the Alires crept into his room. He was as shrunken as a mummy in the hospital bed, and white as the sheets covering him up to his chin. An IV ran from his bone-thin arm to a suspended glucose bag. Wires ran from his chest to a heart monitor that beeped continually. He opened his eyes.

"Hi, Flip, it's us," said Adán. "Me, Rosealba, Luli. Can you hear us?"

Flip looked around, bewildered, blinking.

"You're in the hospital. We're with you, amigo. Hang in there, old buddy."

Flip closed his eyes and fell asleep.

Luli called Jean-Luc that evening. "You probably don't want to hear this, but for what it's worth, your father's in the hospital. The doctor who's been seeing him doesn't think he'll make it this time. I thought you should know."

There was a long silence on the line, the sub-oceanic connection interrupted by periodic static, a whooshing sound, pings, and echoes.

"Jean-Luc? Are you there?"

She heard a deep sigh. "Yes, I'm here. Thank you for calling. I'll talk to you soon," he said, and hung up.

It was touch and go with Flip. Luli and the Alires visited him every day. To their surprise, and Doctor Pacheco's, he grew stronger. Soon, he was sitting up in bed. He thanked his visitors for their attention. "I'll be back at my post in no time," he said feebly. "I certainly hope the newspaper hasn't given away my spot to someone else. It's a hot corner for sales."

He began to cough uncontrollably, spitting up blood.

"I think you'd better leave," Dr. Pacheco said.

Through the kitchen window Luli saw a small red car with an Avis license plate park in her driveway. She wiped her hands on a dishtowel and walked to the front of the house just as someone knocked.

At first, she didn't recognize the handsome stranger standing on her stoop, a tall, tanned man wearing a Panama hat low on his brow, sunglasses, a pale blue Lacoste shirt, and pressed khakis. Like a bolt of lightning, she realized who it was. She threw open the screen door and wordlessly, she and Jean-Luc wound their arms around each other tightly.

In honor of her guest, Luli called in sick to her jobs for the following day. Only Mrs. Stoss seemed to care. "I told you at the outset that I need you to be reliable," she said in a loud, angry voice. "I'm having important people from the opera to dinner tomorrow night. I want this house to be spotless. This is no time for you to be sick!"

Jean-Luc, standing beside Luli, heard Mrs. Stoss's rant. He grinned mischievously. With two fingers he made a throat-slitting gesture.

"Mrs. Stoss," Luli said, her eyes twinkling, "Allow me to point out that you don't own me. I don't work on your plantation, honey, not even for your stingy $10 an hour. Besides, you're a cheapskate, a pretentious, neurotic, self-absorbed, crashing . . . puta cabrona. You are fired!"

She slammed the phone down. "And you . . ." she wagged a finger at Jean-Luc, "are a terrible influence!"

"Of course I am!" he said, laughing. "Now that you're liberated, may I have the grand tour of the Château Luli? I've never been in an authentic adobe before. Well, maybe in Africa, but those were poor people's homes, very humble."

"From what I understand, adobes here in New Mexico were also poor people's homes, but these days they mostly belong to the rich."

"It's a wonderful house. Plenty of light."

"I love it. Aside from being free, it's cozy and plenty roomy for me. It stays pretty cool in the summer and keeps heat in now that it's chilly. And I'm thrilled to live next door to the Alires."

Jean-Luc browsed the books in the living room. "This guy's pretty well read—in English and in French."

"He's a writer. And something of a Francophile, I gather."

"He has great taste in art. These watercolors are lovely."

Luli blushed but said nothing.

"Don't you like them? The color sense is remarkably sophisticated and they are gorgeously painted. They fit perfectly in this place. They look as if they are all by the same person. Must be worth a bundle, although it's sort of surprising he hasn't bothered to frame them. Are they the owner's work?"

Her eyes lit up, and a little smile tugged at the corners of her mouth. But she remained silent.

Jean-Luc was mystified. He looked from Luli to the paintings, then back again to her. Finally, he understood. "Oh, my God. These are *yours*? Bon Jesú! I'm very impressed, Mrs. Russell."

"Merci, Monsieur Phillips. You know, I tried to take courses after I married, but Herb did everything possible to keep me from pursuing my dream."

"He was probably jealous of your creative streak, of talent he doesn't have. You've been hiding your light under a bushel for too long, madame."

The following morning there was a knock shortly after Luli stepped into the shower. Jean Luc opened the front door to a small woman wearing an apron. "I'm going to guess you are the famous Rosealba," he said.

"Not so famous. You're Flip's son, Luc?"

"A sus órdenes, Señora Alire. Please come in." He showed her into the living room.

She sat down on the edge of the sofa. "I want invite you and Luli to dinner."

"Thank you. Luli says you're a fabulous cook."

"No, no. I made carne adovada, and I have much more than we need. Can you eat chile?"

"I love chile. I spent a while in Mexico and I'm addicted to picante."

"Well, this isn't very hot. It's pork baked in red chile."

"Fabuloso. I can contribute some guacamole, if you want. We have a couple of ripe avocadoes on hand."

"Adán loves that stuff. So do I. You know how to make it?"

"I do. Guacamole's on my sailboat's menu almost daily. One of my passengers' favorites."

"Bueno, see you around six-thirty, Mr. Jean-Luc?"

"Si, señora. I will tell la Señora Luli. ¡Muchas gracias!"

After dinner, Luli and Jean-Luc lay in bed holding each other.

"That was the best meal I've had in years," Luc said.

"Me, too. I'm getting to be a chile lover myself. Midwest cooking is so bland by comparison to New Mexican."

"French food as well." He kissed her. "The Alires are lovely people, and they're very fond of you."

"They're the best."

They talked late into the night. Eventually, the conversation turned to Flip. Even in the dark, Luli sensed Jean-Luc become agitated. She let him vent.

"I don't know if I can bear the sight of that son of a bitch," he told her. "When I think of all the times he let us down, let *me* down, I think I'll detonate. The worst is that he couldn't even make the occasional effort to know me and my family."

"He's an old man now, a bag of bones, a featherless, tiny sparrow, barely warm."

"He could be a puddle of piss, for all I care. I still hate him for what he did to my family. I'm sorry. You must think I'm a heartless bastard."

"Of course not. I completely understand. By the time my father was dying, I felt nothing for him. He was an intelligent, creative, talented man who wasted his whole life on booze. He caused my brothers, my mother, and me incredible heartache. Being a dutiful daughter, I went through the motions of helping take care of him. Gradually, my anger seemed to dissipate, like the fizz going out of a bottle of Coke, leaving it flat and tasteless. He was too pitiful to hate. He genuinely appreciated the care we gave him. He even tried to apologize to me, Brad, my mother. But he never could quite wrap his mouth around the words 'I'm sorry.'"

"I don't want anything from Father. Basically, I came here to see you."

"Really?" Luli was shocked.

"Yes, really. I'm not even sure I want to visit him."

The next day, however, Jean-Luc announced he would see Flip. "What the hell," he said with resignation.

As they walked down the hospital corridor toward the intensive care unit, Luli held Jean-Luc's hand. He was fidgety and his hands were sweating. Dr. Pacheco, her white coat flying, raced out of the ICU and stopped when she saw them.

"Dr. Pacheco, this is Jean-Luc Phillips, Flip's son."

Inés shook his hand and held it for a bit. "I'm sorry you couldn't make it here sooner," she said soberly.

"Is he . . . did he . . .?" Luli asked, choking on her words.

"No, he's not dead. He's out of the ICU and in his old room, in fact. He's made a remarkable recovery, at least physically, although I don't expect it to last long. I have to run, but come to my office after you see him and I'll explain."

Although the door to Flip's room was open, Luli rapped on it.

"Come in," Flip said in a faint, raspy voice.

"Hi, Flip. I brought someone special for you to see."

Jean-Luc peered our from behind her, with his hands clasped together looking like an errant schoolboy called into the principal's office.

Flip glanced at him, then looked away. "Please have a seat. Are you here to read to me?"

"No, not today. We're here to see how you're doing. I've been coming every day, sometimes with Adán and Rosealba."

"Forgive me, I don't believe I've been introduced to the people you're referring to." He looked from Luli to Jean-Luc, then back to Luli. "Do I know you?" Then he answered his own question. "Of course I do. Please excuse my forgetfulness. I've been out of town. In Switzerland on business, as a matter of fact. Visiting my brokerage firm's Geneva office. Jet lag can leave one quite confused, you know, even when you're traveling in your own plane."

Luli was bewildered. "Uh, Flip? It's me, Luli Russell."

"Yes, yes. I remember. You work in this hotel. I certainly do remember you. You read me the market report from *The Wall Street Journal*—yesterday, wasn't it? We met in the bar. It was so dark I couldn't see to read my paper.

"Now, who's this young man? Are you a waiter? You look rather familiar. Have you waited on me before? Maybe you could bring me a drink. A Myers's and soda. I'd appreciate it. I'm a big tipper. I'll make it worth your while."

Turning on his heel, Jean-Luc left the room.

Dr. Pacheco invited them into her office and closed the door behind them. "I'm so sorry. He was doing well on the latest round of vitamin B-1 therapy, but then overnight, his computer screen went blank."

Jean-Luc and Luli looked at each other, puzzled.

"Allow me to explain. Flip has descended into what's known as Korsakoff's Syndrome. It's fairly common in end-stage alcoholics, a sudden memory loss brought on by a thiamine deficiency—malnutrition. It's not unlike a computer crash. I know my aunt and uncle took great care of him, and so did you. All of you tried to feed him the best diet possible, but it was no use. He couldn't stay away from the alcohol, in spite of everyone's best efforts."

"Can you explain more about this syndrome?" Luli asked.

"Sure. Basically, his short-term memory is completely shot, although he may still have traces of his long-term memory. Did he know who you are?" she asked Jean-Luc.

"Not really. I mean, there was maybe a nanosecond of recognition, but I could have imagined it. He thought I was a waiter. Asked me to bring him a drink. Promised me a good tip," Jean-Luc laughed bitterly.

"It's sad you couldn't have gotten here before this happened. He's gone. He will probably live for a while longer, although his liver is in terrible shape, and his heart condition is worsening. But he won't recognize anyone, not even family or friends. Even if you go out of the room and come right back in, he will forget your visit. He'll also confabulate—make up grandiose schemes about who he is, and where he is."

"He thinks he's in a hotel," Luli said. "Just returned from a trip to his brokerage office in Switzerland."

Dr. Pacheco gave a little laugh. "Well, this place ain't exactly the Ritz. We'll do our best for him. If he continues to improve physically, I'll suggest moving him to a nursing home. I know Rosealba and Adán will want to care for him, but it would be too much for them. He'll need 'round the clock skilled nursing. I'll insist."

32

· · · · · · ·

LULI AND JEAN-LUC SAT AT HER KITCHEN TABLE,
sharing a supper of steamed tamales and salad.

"How does this feel to you?" Luli asked. "Your father's
being mentally gone?"

"Well, he's been gone a long time, so this isn't exactly
new for me. I didn't think I ever wanted him to come back,
but Sarah thought that somewhere in my heart of hearts, I
did. She'd see a certain glazed look in my eye, and tell me to
give it up. Her point was if I harbored even the tiniest bit of
hope of a reconciliation, it would only prolong the loss I'd
suffered years before."

"Smart lady."

Jean-Luc stayed quiet for a few seconds, then reached
across the table, kissed Luli, and cupped her face in his
hands. "I never thought I'd fall in love again. But I have.
I'm wild about you, Luli. From that first hour in the cistern,
there was this easy intimacy. It baffles me."

"I think you just like to beat me at Scrabble," she teased.

In spite of their sorrow about Flip, Jean-Luc and Luli made love for the first time that night. "Is this inappropriate?" Jean-Luc asked, as they slowly began removing one another's clothes, letting them fall to the floor.

"If it seems right to you, it seems right to me, like ... maybe this is life affirming. If it doesn't sound too woo-woo, too Santa Fe to you?"

"No, ma chérie. Here we are at long last, shedding clothes as if they were bad habits."

"Yes!" She flung off her remaining clothing, wrapped her arms around him, and danced him backwards toward her bedroom. "You do know where this is going, don't you?"

Jean-Luc looked down at his naked self. "Hmmmm. Don't think there's any going anywhere else except to bed with you. I've been thinking about this for a long time."

"Me, too. But it's good I had some wine with dinner," she said as they dropped into bed. "I'm kinda nervous; I'm a little out of practice, you know."

Jean-Luc put a finger to her lips and kissed her, his mouth blending with hers, his hands exploring her, guiding her hands to discover him. "No apologies allowed," he said when they came up briefly for air before resuming the meshing of their limbs, the cruising of each others' bodies with hands, lips, tongues.

Luli found herself giggling.

Jean-Luc leaned back on the pillows, his brow furrowed. In a thick faux French accent, he said, "Madame, may I remind you that we Frenchmen are famous as skilled and ardent lovers," he teased, bringing her face to his. "Some-zing is funny?"

"Somezing is *wonderful*. I'm feeling all tingly. Oh, my God. Here I am, fifty years old with four children, but I feel like I've never made love before."

Luli woke first. She rolled over, curled into his side, and began stroking his unshaven cheek. Jean-Luc lifted one eyelid. "Am I where I think I am? Where I hope I am?" he asked.

"Monsieur, you are absolutely in the right place. Moi, I'm in total heaven. I have never felt so splendid in my entire life."

Jean-Luc grinned. "Moi non plus. You said you were out of practice, but you could have fooled me." He pulled her closer. "Ma chérie—perhaps we should work on our proficiency?"

When they woke again, Luli snuggled deeper into his arms. "I must tell you, if you're any example, those rumors about French lovers are true. "Bundan iyisi, Şam'da kayısı!"

"Comment?"

"It's Turkish, means . . . the only thing better than this is an apricot from Damascus."

Jean-Luc grinned. "I've actually eaten apricots in Syria. They're pretty damn tasty. But you, my dear, you're much, much more delicious."

They sat by the dining room window taking in the panorama of the city below, enjoying a continental breakfast, leaning over the table to kiss now and then and stare at each other in wonder.

"This is glorious," Jean-Luc said, taking in the view. "I haven't seen autumn in a long time, living in the tropics. I forgot how brilliant the colors are."

"The palette here is more lemon yellows and ochres than in the Midwest and the Northeast, with all those brilliant flame red and cadmium orange maples and oaks."

"Spoken like a true painter," Jean-Luc said. "Say, this jam is wonderful. Apricot?"

"Yes. With fruit from Rosealba's tree. We made it in late July. I think I told you about that."

"Ah, yes, the fabled jam session."

"We put up sixty-three jars."

"That's a lot of jam. You Santa Feans are big into apricots."

"There's only a crop maybe every five years because a freeze often zaps the trees, so you have to make the best of a rare opportunity. Still, everyone in this town seems to have at least one apricot tree. In spring, when I first met the Alires and their tree was in bloom, Rosealba promised me this would be an apricot year."

"People here must be optimists."

"We are."

Jean-Luc took another bite of his toast. "Tell me the Turkish phrase again."

" Bundan iyisi, Şam'da kayısı," Luli laughed.

At first, Jean-Luc refused to go back to the hospital. He went for long walks by himself in the foothills of the Sangres. Sometimes Luli went with him. He seemed to be brooding, walking with his head down, his hands in his pockets. She never insisted he visit his father.

He came home from a long hike up the Atalaya Trail. "OK, I can see him now," he announced with a huge sigh.

He began to visit Flip every day while Luli cleaned house for her remaining customers. He'd read him the newspapers, try to talk to him about Eugènie, his granddaughters, Ste. Foi, in the hope that Flip's long-term memory might kick in. But it was useless. Flip wasn't interested. He never recognized his son—or Luli or the Alires. Each time they came to see him he thought his visitors were different people. He appreciated their solicitousness. Sometimes he thought he was at the Georges V in Paris, or the Hotel Kempinski in Berlin, or the Waldorf Astoria. Sometimes he was home in his Manhattan apartment. He was never in the Maison Azure on Ste. Foi, nor did he mention Santa Fe.

Luli showed Jean-Luc around town when she had free time. "Let's walk down to the Plaza," she said on a sunny Saturday. "I want to show you the Museum of Fine Arts. It's one of my favorite spots. I go there as often as I can."

They crossed the Plaza, arm in arm. A gaggle of young men and girls, most of them sporting Rasta ringlets and tattoos, kicked a hacky sack around their circle. Despite the fall chill, families perched on the low wall surrounding the obelisk in the middle of the square licking ice cream cones. A bedraggled man with a long beard sat hunched over a guitar on a park bench, playing and muttering a song to himself, his spotted dog lying on the dry grass beside him.

"Will you look at that!" Jean-Luc said, pointing to the sleeping dog. On its back lay a gray cat, also dozing, and resting on top of the cat was a mouse.

"Fabulous!" Luli walked over to the man and dropped a couple of dollars into his coffee can. He gave her a gap-toothed grin and kept strumming.

Under the portal of the Palace of the Governors they cruised the line of Indian vendors who bantered busily with customers. Their handmade jewelry lay spread out on blankets, silver and turquoise gleaming in the sun.

The museum, a solid block of stuccoed adobe and heavy beams, took up most of the northwest corner of Lincoln and Palace.

"Handsome building," Jean-Luc said when they walked inside.

"It dates from 1917. The design is based on the church at Acoma. Some people think this structure started the Pueblo revival style which is the primary architectural influence in Santa Fe."

"All that soft-edged brown adobe?"

"It's everywhere."

While Jean-Luc paid for their tickets, Luli read the listing of current exhibits. "Aha! We're in luck. The Gustave Baumann show is still up."

She took Jean-Luc's hand and led him upstairs. "I love this artist. He's best known for his Southwest woodcuts. I would never have the patience to master the medium, but I admire his work."

"Très bien," Jean Luc said, inspecting the step-by-step phases of a print, from Baumann's gouache studies, to carved blocks of wood, to single color proofs, to the finished piece. "A German. Why am I not surprised? This is an art form they've excelled at since before Dürer."

"Aren't his colors amazing? And there's clearly an influence of Japanese prints in the flatness and the clarity of the lines."

"Beats me. I'm a sailor, madame, not a connoisseur. But I know beauty when I see it." He kissed her lightly.

"Come. I want to show you this O'Keeffe." Luli beckoned him around the corner to a painting of spring cottonwoods sprouting splotches of yellow green. "She doesn't have the control Baumann has, but the work is more exuberant, much more free."

"She was rumored to be a free spirit, after all."

"Truth is, I'm not wild about a lot of her work."

"Heresy, madame! Don't all women artists long to be La Georgia?"

"Not me. She lived an interesting life, and she was one of only a handful of women artists to receive recognition in her era. But I think the adulation is way overdone."

"I can see why you love this museum, though. It's a lot like Santa Fe itself. Small but of very high quality. This town certainly has a wealth of amenities: amazing food, concerts, museums, galleries. I love the mountains. I think I'd miss the water, though."

"Well, all this used to be an ocean. Except we're a few million years late."

They grew closer, finding they enjoyed the same things, realizing they could communicate without words. They enjoyed making slow, patient love, attentive to each other. But Jean-Luc couldn't escape a profound sadness.

"I don't think I'll really get past the hurt until Flip's gone. I can't explain it."

"You don't have to."

She wasn't surprised when Luc announced he was returning to the island. "I have to go back to the marina. But I want us to be together, Luli."

"Yes, but something tells me this is not the right time."

He nodded glumly. "We'll work it out somehow."

"I know we will."

Luli missed Jean-Luc terribly. She bought a computer so they could communicate via the Internet, rationalizing the purchase as a necessity for her accounting class that required her to learn QuickBooks and Excel. She made new friends at school, and began to go out more. She often stopped by Perspective, the gallery where Savannah worked. They'd go to movies or to Canyon Road openings where Savannah introduced her to artists and members of their community.

Whenever she had free time, Luli painted. Abstracted clouds, sunsets, tortured juniper trees, desert wildflowers, vague camouflaged deer slipping through a forest, cutthroat trout glinting in a sunlit mountain stream. Other than her late-night chats with Jean-Luc, making art was one of the few aspects of her life that made her truly happy. When she was painting, she had no idea what day it was, or what time it was; she was never hungry or thirsty. She was simply lost in her communication with her colors, her brushes, and the images she wanted to lay down on paper.

Luli joined Savannah and her boss, Jules, on a Friday night "arts crawl" when most galleries stayed open later, some serving wine and finger food. She'd never spent much time with him, but she found Jules charming.

"Savannah showed me some of your new paintings," he said. "I'm impressed."

"Really? I'm still getting used to the intensity of the light here. It's a real challenge to capture that in watercolors."

Jules shrugged. "Your work is refreshing. It's not the usual 'Hi, I've invented Santa Fe in my marvelous artistic expression, and you owe me homage' we see so often from the arrivistes—both anciens and derniers. But I'm discovering wonderful work from artists who haven't shown here before—like you. In fact, Savannah and I have been talking about putting together a show of work by artists new to Santa Fe. Are you interested?"

"Are you kidding? Of course I'm interested. And extremely flattered!"

Luli phoned Jean-Luc that night. "I hope it's not too late to call."

"Not if it's good news. I'm often up past midnight anyway. So . . . it *is* good news, isn't it?" he asked cautiously.

"It's fabulous news. Perspective, the gallery my friend Savannah manages, is offering me a show with two other artists—a sculptor and a photographer. My first exhibit here."

"I'm not surprised in the least, Luli. Judging from the photos you've been sending me, your work is getting better every time you fill your brush. I like that gallery. It's one of the best in Santa Fe, isn't it?"

"I guess so. It's my favorite, anyway."

"When's the exhibit?"

"The opening's the second Friday in December. Savannah says it'll be a splendid time to catch visitors in town for the holidays and people might be Christmas shopping. That doesn't give me much time to prepare."

"You have a number of finished paintings, don't you?"

"True. But I need more. I hope to have about twenty. They want to use the painting with the gold aspen grove in early snowfall for the announcement postcard and the advertising."

"My favorite—or the one with the deep red Virginia creeper climbing over a crumbling adobe wall. I'm so happy for you. This is a wonderful break!"

Flip was in a rehab center near the hospital. Luli emailed Jean-Luc about him almost daily. "He's like a slowly melting ice cube," she wrote. "Every day, there's a little less of him here on the planet. It's so sad. But I have to tell you, the confabulations Dr. Pacheco warned us about are sometimes hilarious. Today, he mistook me for Wallace Warfield Simpson. He hinted that we'd recently had quite a chummy encounter."

Jean-Luc called minutes after she sent the message. "Say, Wally, how's the Duke?" he laughed. "Tell me something. Were you really worth giving up a throne for?"

"You'd better believe it, dahling."

Luli's cellphone rang one evening as she was coming in from her accounting class. Hoping it was Jean-Luc, she rummaged through her tote bag for it. "Bon soir!" she said cheerfully.

"Huh?" a familiar voice said. "Hey—where the hell have you been? I've been trying to reach you all day."

Still holding the phone, Luli plopped down in an armchair and kicked off her shoes.

The voice barked at her again. "Are you there? Answer me."

Luli sighed. "Herb, aren't you forgetting something? We're divorced. I don't have to answer to you for anything. Good-bye."

"Wait," he said plaintively. "Don't hang up on me. I have to talk to you."

"Is it about the kids? Are they OK?"

"How would I know? They won't talk to me for some reason."

For damn good reasons, Luli thought. "What do you want, Herb? I'm tired. I've had a long day cleaning other people's houses."

"I want you to come home. I'm sorry about that little fling."

"Fling? FLING! What about the part where you cleaned out our bank accounts and caused us to lose our house? My home? Our kids' home?"

"Cut me some slack, Luli. I'm sick. Real sick."

She could hear him sniffling.

Then he began to sob. "I'm sorry for everything. I was a jerk. I need you. It's pancreatic cancer. I'm living in a friend's motel in De Pere."

She greeted his news with silence.

"Are you still there? The doc says I only have a couple of months to live."

Luli instantly thought of a thousand nasty, angry barbs she could hurl at Herb like, "Why doesn't your whore take care of you?" or "All you're really sorry for is yourself." Instead, she said: "Give me your phone number. I'll call you tomorrow," and hung up.

Luli spent a sleepless night. She needed to talk to someone. Maybe Dr. Hirsch could give her an appointment sooner than her regular time slot.

Rosealba noticed Luli was unusually subdued on their drive out to El Dorado where they cleaned a large house together every other week. "What's up, m'ija?"

She told her about Herb's call, breaking into tears.

"Oooh, what a tough one. I know the Bible say we suppose to forgive people and all that, but I'm real sorry, I don't believe in forgiving unforgiveable stuff. Like him taking off with your babysitter, leaving you and your kids without no money, losing your house. If you were the one who ran out on him, and you got cancer, you think he come take care of you?"

"Of course not."

Dr. Hirsch could see Luli the following afternoon. During their meeting, they talked about betrayal, obligations, loyalty, guilt, justice, karma.

"What would it be like if you went to Green Bay to nurse him?"

"Awful. He'd be a difficult, dreadful patient. He always was when he was sick during our marriage. Besides, I have no money. Apparently he has no money, and I don't want to be stuck back in Green Bay."

"How will you feel if you don't go care for him?"

"Same answer—awful."

Their discussion was so intense Luli left Dr. Hirsch's office with her brain buzzing. She didn't call Herb that evening, or the next, going numbly through her daily paces of housecleaning, school, visiting Flip to read to him. She hoped the right decision would pop into her head.

Jean-Luc emailed her. "I know something's wrong. I haven't heard from you in days. I'm here for you. Call me, write me. Whatever it is, I want to know about it."

She sent him the bad news. "My ex has terminal cancer and wants me to return to Green Bay to take care of him. I don't know what to do. I'll call you when I make up my mind."

His reply was one sentence: "I love you."

On the morning of the fourth day after Herb's call, as she was leaving the house to go to work, the phone rang. She dreaded picking it up, certain it was Herb. He'd yell at her, berate her for not calling her, then whine and plead. She let it ring a few times before she answered.

"Hello?" she said dully.

"Luli? It's Jerry Bourgoin, from Green Bay. Is this a good time to talk?"

"I guess so, Jerry. What's up?"

"Well, my boss thought I should be the one to tell you this."

Luli's heart skipped several beats. Now what? Why were the cops calling her? Had something happened to one of the kids? Was Herb in trouble with the law? Had he disgraced himself yet again?

"It's about Herb. He was driving across some tracks north of De Pere early this morning, and his car got hit by a freight train."

She was suddenly very cold.

"Luli? Are you there?"

"I'm here."

"He was dead in an instant. Never knew what hit him."

Luli would always wonder if the accident was an accident, or if Herb had killed himself.

She emailed Jean-Luc.

He responded immediately. "Gather your children, your family, friends, neighbors. Bury him, mourn him. Do whatever you need to do. You know where I am, you know I love you, and I want to be with you. When you're ready, we'll figure out how we can be together."

"I'm still in shock but I'll call you soon. I love you," she replied.

To her surprise, Herb hadn't cashed in his life insurance policy. Even more to her amazement, the insurers paid up, and the bank didn't go after the money. Luli could pay for the funeral, with enough left to cover college costs. In the middle of all the horror, the cash was a blast of sunshine and relief. Ironically, despite the fact that Herb hated her painting, his insurance money paid to frame her work for the exhibit.

The morning of the opening, Savannah called early. "I'm sorry to bother you, today of all days, but both of my assistants are out with the flu. Is there any way you can help hang the show?"

Luli, Savannah, and the other artists worked feverishly. Adán came to hang her paintings. "You just tell me where you want them. Rosealba will come later for the opening. We're so excited for you. We've never been to one of these things before. Rosie and her husband are coming, Sammy and his wife, Inés and her kids. They're all very pleased you invited them."

"I wish Flip could be here," Luli said. "But I know it's not possible."

"Inés says he's failing fast; he could go any time now."

By three, the exhibit was ready. Luli and Savannah set out wine, sparkling water, cookies, fruit, and cheese. "I'm going home to take a shower and put on my finery," Luli announced.

Adán gave her a ride. When they stopped at the top of the hill, Rosie's truck was parked in the driveway, next to her mother's car. "Ooooh, something smells delicious. What are the Rosies cooking?"

Adán shrugged. "You never know what those two are up to."

Shortly before five, Rosealba tapped on Luli's door. "Do you want to drive with us? We can bring you home, too."

At the gallery, a number of people had already arrived, and more were streaming in. Holding plastic cups of wine, they meandered through Perspective's several rooms, stopping to chat or admire the artwork.

As soon as Luli walked in, Savannah raced up to her. "Did you see the red stickers on two of your paintings?" she asked excitedly.

"No. I can't believe it. You've sold two already?"

"Yeah, and to the most gorgeous man I've seen in ages. I think he's even straight. Tall, wonderful tan, suave. He came in right after you left this afternoon, walked up to your paintings, and when I asked if I could help him, he said: 'I'll take those two.'"

"Wow. Just like that?"

"Yes. I don't even know if he looked at anything else."

"Which ones did he buy?"

Savannah led Luli to the wall where her work hung, and pointed out the two with red stickers.

"Ohhhh, those two? I was kinda hoping they wouldn't sell."

"Luli, a sale is a sale. Never put a price tag on something you don't want to part with!"

"Well, normally I would be delighted. But I was thinking of giving those to a friend of mine for Christmas. Did he pay for them?"

"Yes, in cash no less. I suggested he come back after five so he can meet you. Man, he is so handsome. With the most wonderful smile. And no gold band on either ring finger." She glanced toward the door and whispered, "Oh, my God. Here he is! Isn't he absolutely divine?"

Luli took one look at the man and slid to the floor.

It was almost 7:30 by the time Adán parked on Alire Circle and everyone got out of the car. Brown paper lunch bags with candles flickering inside them edged both sides of the walkway to the door. "What is this?" Luli asked Rosealba.

"Farolitos. Usually we only put them out at Christmas, you know, to lead the Baby Jesus to our house. But this is a special occasion. It was Adán's idea."

"They're so pretty! But aren't the bags going to catch on fire?"

"No. You put little round candles in sand at the bottom of the bag so they don't fall against the paper," Adán explained.

"Please come inside for a snack," Rosealba said, her eyes alive and merry.

When Luli walked in, she was stunned to find the other

artists, Savannah, Jules, Sammy, Inés, and friends waiting in the Alire's living room. A feast covered the kitchen table: savory empanadas, red chile enchiladas, enchiladas suizas, carne adovada, homemade flour tortillas, salads, guacamole, tortilla chips, agua de sandía, and for dessert, apricot pies with whipped cream.

"Oh, Rosies! This is muy fabuloso. You shouldn't have gone to all this trouble."

Rosealba shrugged. "Of course we'd do this for you, m'ija. Rosita helped me, and Adán. He never tells anybody, but his tortillas are better than mine. We even put Jean-Luc to work. That man sure knows his way around a kitchen. You should see him chop onions—exactly like them TV chefs. Adán taught him his secret chile colorado recipe. It's the best."

"A very important life skill. Now he has to teach me."

More guests arrived, filling the Alire's small house with happy, noisy, partygoers. The food was quickly dished up onto paper plates. The Alires were engulfed in praise for their cooking.

"What a feed!" Samantha gushed, twirling her fork in the air. "This is the yummiest New Mexican food ever."

"This is the best any kind of food," Jules corrected her.

"It's beyond delicious," Luli said. "Adán, Rosealba, Rosie, and you, Luc—how can I ever thank you enough? This is the most wonderful fiesta imaginable."

As the food gave out, Rosita and friends pitched in to clean up the kitchen until it shone and everything had been put away. Guests began to leave, keeping the cooks busy at the door with profuse thanks and good-byes. The Alires, Jean-Luc, and Luli were thoroughly exhausted by the time the last one left. They stood in a bone-tired clump in the living room, their arms around one another's shoulders as if propping each other up.

"Did you know Luc was coming for the opening?" Luli asked Rosealba.

"Of course! He call us right after you tell him about the exhibit. But he want to keep it a secret."

"Quel enfant terrible, Jean-Luc!"

He winked at Rosealba and Adán. "Luli thinks I'm a bad boy."

"No, hija," Rosealba said, shaking her head. "He's no malcriado. He don't want you to know he's coming. He want to surprise you."

"Well, he sure did. I almost had a heart attack."

"I wouldn't have missed this for the world," Luc said.

"The feast or the exhibit?" Luli asked with a wry grin.

Jean-Luc kissed Luli's cheek. "Why, ma chérie, the Rosies' cooking, of course."

Acknowledgments

. . . .

A HEAVENLY HOST OF HELPERS MADE *AN APRICOT Year* a reality. Please bear in mind that the elderly author and her almost as elderly editor have surely forgotten to include many wonderful souls who lent a hand with this book. If your contribution has been overlooked, it is amnesia at work rather than spite—OK, Frank?

Carol Eastes gets a galaxy of gold stars on her report card for the swell job she has done as the Editor & Chief of Papalote Press these past seven years. She is especially invaluable to me for insisting I slow down and write better. It is she who wields the dreaded Red Pen of Death, endlessly slashing and burning my manuscripts. The wonderful author photograph, taken in a quinoa field in Ollantaytambo, Peru, is her work, too. She has been a paragon of patience, and a good sport, even letting me win at Scrabble once in a while. You are the best, chica!

Laura Burns, editor extraordinaire, supplied insights about sailors and hurricanes, and unearthed even more mistakes in the manuscript. Brava!

Many thanks to Ann Baumann and The New Mexico Museum of Art for permission to use *The Bishop's Apricot* as the cover image of this book, and to Gustave Baumann for his glorious prints. Thanks to Michelle Gallagher Roberts for helping us obtain the rights.

Much love to Kate Krasin, a fabulous printmaker who spent one of her last afternoons on the planet advising us on artwork for the cover.

Piropos to Denise Chávez, who leads the parade, and to Winn Bundy, who bakes the cakes. Both of these extraordinary book people have done so much over the years for authors and readers of all ages.

A thousand thanks to Barbara Haines who once again has designed a beautiful book with patience and grace, maintaining her sense of humor even in the dark and scary places.

Thanks to our publicist Michael Hice, who fully intends to make me even more famous as soon as he possibly can.

¡Muchisimas gracias! to the Pachamamas: Lolly Martin, Donna Herring, Mary Berkeley, and Bill Farmer. They keep the wheels turning at Pachamama, my thirty-eight-year old folk art gallery. Together with organizational assistants Cheryl Bass, Noel Chilton, Zoila Cleaver, and Rosario Fiallos, my helpers make it possible for me to dedicate my time to writing.

Many thanks to Drs. Barbara Hanke, Grant LaFarge, Barbara Hummel-Joesten, and Will MacHendrie for helping me understand terminal alcoholism. Thanks to John Blanchard at Artisan for his excellent advice on brushes and watercolors.

Merci beaucoup to my French-speaking consultants, Patricia Stelzner and Tim Egan. Mil gracias to my Spanish-speaking advisors, Sam Adelo, Frances Miller de Echeverría, Hammer, and Juan Cabrero Oliver. Thanks to the ever talented Kathy Chilton for help with the Turkish and for the lovely drawings of apricots. To readers Gail Rieke, Melissa Martínez, and Winn Bundy, gratitude for your time and suggestions.

And last but not least, I am indebted to UNM Press for distributing my books, and to bookstore staff everywhere who get my work into the hands of readers.

¡¡¡You rock, mi gente!!!

Martha Egan
Corrales, NM

At the tender age of sixty, Martha Egan began a new career in fiction with *Clearing Customs*, based on her experiences as an importer. *OnLine Review of Books and Current Affairs* named the novel Fiction Book of the Year in 2005. Her next books, *Coyota* and *La Ranfla & Other New Mexico Stories*, won Bronze Ippy Awards for Mountain-West Regional Fiction.

Egan owns Pachamama, a Santa Fe gallery specializing in Latin American folk art and antiques. She has authored two nonfiction books, *Milagros: Votive Offerings from the Americas* and *Relicarios: Devotional Miniatures from the Americas*, both published by the Museum of New Mexico Press.

A rabid Green Bay Packers fan and stockholder, she is Tia Marta to four dozen nieces and nephews. She divides her time between toy stores in Corrales and Santa Fe, New Mexico, and Egg Harbor, Wisconsin.

Printed in the USA
Editor: Carol Eastes
Design: Barbara Haines
Composed in Garamond Premier Pro text with Ragged Write display